Jürgen Heimlich

# The Mystery of Willoughby

## The unsolved case of "the Girl in Blue"

Translated from German by
Christina Römer

Jürgen Heimlich

# The Mystery of Willoughby

The unsolved case of
"the Girl in Blue"

Bibliografic information of the German National Library:

*Die Deutsche Nationalbibliothek verzeichnet diese Publikation in der Deutschen Nationalbibliografie; detaillierte bibliografische Daten sind im Internet über http://dnb.dnb.de abrufbar.*

*TWENTYSIX – Der Self-Publishing-Verlag*
A cooperation between Random House and BoD – Books on Demand

© 2018 Jürgen Heimlich

*Cover painting copyright © 2017 by Elisabeth Kerz*

Production and publishing:

*BoD – Books on Demand, Norderstedt*

ISBN: 9783740748869

Original title: Das Geheimnis von Willoughby

First published  2015 by Eclipse books

# CONTENTS

## ACCIDENT                                                                              9

| | |
|---|---|
| The narrator, 2013 | 10 |
| The Stranger, 1933 | 12 |
| A European in Willoughby, 2013 | 14 |
| A Girl, 1933 | 18 |
| The Doctor, 1933 | 20 |
| The Girl as a young Woman, 1940 | 22 |
| The Hobo, 1933 | 25 |
| The Girl as a young Woman, 1940 | 27 |
| The Doctor, 1933 | 30 |
| A European in Willoughby, 2013 | 32 |
| FIRST PROTOCOL | 36 |
| The Stranger, 1933 | 38 |
| The Doctor, 1933 | 40 |
| The Girl as a young Woman, 1940 | 44 |
| The Stranger, 1933 | 48 |
| Will, the Hobo, 1934 | 51 |
| The Narrator, 2013 | 55 |
| The Girl as a young Woman, 1942 | 59 |
| A European in Willoughby, 2013 | 62 |

## FAREWELL                                 **67**

1933/12/25, Diary of the Mortician          67
The girl as a Young Woman, 1945             71
The Stranger, 1933                          75
1933/12/26, Diary of the Mortician          79
Will, the Hobo, 1933                        82
1933/12/29, Diary of the Mortician          86

SECOND PROTOCOL                             89

The Narrator, 2013                          91
The Girl as a young Woman, 1946             95
The Stranger, 1934                          99
A European in Willoughby, 2013              103
1934/01/07, Diary of the Moritician         107

## MAGIC                                           **111**

Karen, 1963                                       112

Walter, the Actor, recounts (1963)                115

The Narrator, 2013                                119

The Doctor tells his story (1963)                 123

James, the Mortician, recounts (1963)             127

A European in Willoughby, 2013                    132


THIRD PROTOCOL                                    135


Will, the literary scholar, recounts (1963)       137

Karen, the Writer, remembers (1963)               141

A Euoropean in Willoughby, 2013                   145

The Narrator, 2013                                147

Carl talks about the

magic of Willoughby, 2001                         150

*In remembrance of Josephine Klimczak*

# Accident

*The fate of the „Girl in Blue" had instantly fascinated me when I first heard of it. I could never let go of it. I wanted, with every fibre of my soul, that her history to be written down and presented to an interested readership. It took a few years until I found an older man as the suitable narrator who was willing to confront the myth. He is not an easy-going fellow and insisted on putting himself a little in the limelight, too. And thus, our novel starts with its re-entry into the whole wide world of a writer.*

# The Narrator, 2013

It is time. Time to dare wipe the slate clean. Time to finally be overwhelmed by emotions again that will beam me to different spheres. Time to wave to the past and to welcome the present. I don't have much time left. Time to realize the project of my life. ´Are you off your rocker?´ a friend asked me, just as if it was a statement. I didn't answer. After all, I must take my time.

Not to put every word, every question in the balance. At my age, yes especially at my age it is time to rid myself of unnecessary ballast. I have wasted too much time during my life.

Now then here I sit and write. I have done this countless times. Of all things, only writing has granted me lasting moments of pleasure. Once the manuscript was finished, I never was satisfied. There was always a flaw, something that irritated me. Dozens of novels are stashed in my cellar, just one of them I have ever showed to my best friend. No one knows what slumbers in my cellar. Why haven't I tried to exploit the thousands upon thousands of pages? I haven't felt called to address the public. Because actually these novels always dealt with me and my emotional sensitivities. This is now over, once and for all. Writing may have a therapeutical aspect, but not exclusively so.

So I'm daring the leap. I am daring to enter the reality of existence. I am writing reality, because I am sick and tired of deceptiveness. All my life I have sold things that no one needed. I grew rich on that. So rich that I could afford to get myself this house with cellar. In my spare time, I got around to getting even with myself. I had piled so much guilt upon my shoulders. I would never be able to pay off this guilt. Therefore, I wrote about my trespasses, grotesque weaknesses, sad events that I subjected other people to. In my egotism, I ran over everything. No one could be safe from me. It would have been terrible to confront my own fears.

I have spared myself far too long. But that's unbearable in the long run. I am ready to lead the life I have always been ashamed of. The way to myself leads over the You. I am looking into the mirror without smashing it. It is time to forgive myself and to trust myself.

*On a beautiful pre-Christmas day, a citizen of Willoughby was travelling home by bus. Through means of a notebook leaked to me it is possible to be confronted with his innermost thoughts that linked him to the girl in no time at all. The narrator managed the balancing act of empathizing with a past that goes back 80 years.*

## The Stranger, 1933

She stood there with her pouch and smiled at me when I stepped closer to her. ´All alone on your way?´ Her smile was enchanting. She patted her pouch. ´This is all I need´. I didn't want to leave her, but she vanished. She only re-appeared again shortly before the bus continued its journey. She was beaming with pleasure, something must have happened to make her glow like this. The rest of the ride I brooded about how I could hook up with this young, gorgeous woman. We were all going to Willoughby, that little city. I lived there, but the woman must be from out of town. What did she want in this small place? Did it have something to do with the mysterious contents of her pouch?

After four to five hours the bus finally stopped in Willoughby. My legs had gone to sleep from sitting so long. It took a while until I could approach my native soil with steady steps. I almost believed I had lost the girl forever from my sight when I saw her, dragging a big suitcase, not 50 yards away from me as she rounded a corner. Having only a sports bag to carry, I legged it and ran in the direction where I presumed her to be. She was not there. Had she perhaps already arrived at her lodgings? The neighbourhood was familiar to me, but where would the young lady spend the next days, as I was hoping she would?

My heart leapt into my throat! She had returned, was smiling at me with beautiful hazel eyes. ´What a surprise!´

I noticed she was carrying only her pouch. Therefore, she must have found rooms at Mrs. Judd's. A simple accommodation, but with a nice front to look at. ´You'll have to excuse me, I have to take care of something that cannot be postponed. I'm in a hurry!´ She gave me a delightful smile and I looked after her until she had turned into a silhouette. For the rest of the day, I could only think of her. All my life I had never met a creature like her. And I had no idea how long she would remain in Willoughby. I resigned myself to a sleepless night.

*As fate has it, I am not the only one interested in reconstructing the destiny of the "Girl in Blue". A fellow countryman, Austrian, even Viennese like me, was likewise magically drawn to this girl. 80 years after the accident he traveled to Willoughby to investigate what circumstances may have preceded the girl's death. He hoped to track down eyewitnesses. Fortunately, he accepted the invitation of a man who had important information about the events of that day before Christmas of 1933 and beyond.*

## A European in Willoughby, 2013

I'm looking at my watch every few minutes. I consider what I will ask the man. And I am asking myself if I haven't pondered that often enough already. My journey has led me from Vienna this far. The last few yards won't kill me. I must have dozed off for a little while. I'm being shaken rather roughly by the shoulder. I'm rubbing that little sleep from my eyes and look at the bus driver, who is pointing at the exit with his right hand. I nod.

´Good evening!´ The man is very tall and looks young at heart. He's wearing casual clothes. On the way to his apartment we only exchange a few words. I'm getting more nervous by the second. Finally, we're sitting in a nicely furnished room. A middle-aged woman is putting a pot of coffee and cake on the table.

´Well, now we're seeing each other personally for the first time, it's a pleasure!´

He's pouring coffee, handing me a piece of cake.

´Wife made it herself!´

I can't hide my embarrassment.

´Mr. Keanes, I'm much obliged to you for offering me your hospitality for a few days. Be assured that I much appreciate it. After all it won't be long until Christmas. You'll surely have a lot of stress so shortly before the holidays.´

He's smiling mischievously. ´The kids have long left the nest and we will spend the festive season in cosy comfort. Don't you worry.´ For a few seconds, there's an eerie silence.

´You've told me a few things in your email that I simply couldn't believe. Up to now I only know those documents that you were kind enough to provide me with. A few reports from witnesses, general notes, keywords, photos. But that you're the grandson of the doctor who...´

Mr. Keanes clears his throat. ´I grant you that I didn't want to admit to that. Being involved in the affair myself, even if from a great distance. My grandfather kept silent towards me until he fell severely ill. Then he approached me, murmured that under no circumstances should I tell grandmother of my knowledge. I promised and then he narrated the events. He was called to the site of the accident around 11pm. He examined the young woman as she lay on the forest floor like a doll. No external injuries were visible. It seemed as if she was asleep. But she was dead. He convinced himself of that within a few seconds. All around him heated discussions took place. Nobody knew the woman. She had arrived in Willoughby a few hours before. She had taken up lodgings at Mrs. Judd's. As beautiful as an angel, only the wings were missing! My grandfather stated curtly that she must have been touched by the train. A few witnesses confirmed this. They had noticed how the young woman had run to meet the train. It was incomprehensible to them how it could have happened that she came into direct contact with it. Was it a moment of carelessness that claimed this unknown young woman's life? Or had it been her voluntary decision to depart this life? No one knew the answer to that, not even the doctor. There was nothing he could do for her anymore. Third party negligence could be ruled out. At that time of the day, there were almost no people out and about and those few that were didn't linger close to the station but mostly made their way to the Christmas Eve midnight Mass. The train could have taken the young woman to New York. Perhaps she had business there, it was rumored. My grandfather certified the death and stated as cause of death that she had been fatally brushed by a train. Maybe she had just been accidentally hurled into the forested area and had broken her neck. He had seen the young woman leave Mrs. Judd's pension just a few minutes after her arrival. So, she must have had something to do in Willoughby. Afterwards there had been reports that she had lain down to sleep immediately, tired from the long journey, and had gone to church a little later. But that can't be proved with certainty. The truth isn't that easy to discover.

No one wanted to reconstruct what happened in the span of those few hours, and neither did my grandfather. He confessed to his wife as early as the next day that he had fallen in love with the young woman during a brief encounter. A short conversation had sufficed to nearly make him lose his mind. He had to make every possible effort not to burst into tears at the sight of the corpse. This woman had been something very special, he had noticed that immediately. She wasn't just as pretty as a picture, but also graced with a pure heart. She had looked into his heart, he told me. Straight into the heart and then he had heard all angels sing.´

That evening Mr. Keanes told for hours how his grandfather suffered his whole life from having given his heart to a deceased. He did not neglect his wife, but inwardly he was closer to the dead woman than to any human soul.

*The European kept leafing through the records and written statements. Prior to his stay in Willoughby he occupied himself with it whole nights through. This evening too, being right at the scene of the incident, he rummaged around in his traveling bag for the documents, to recall the time when the "Girl in Blue" seemed to enchant the town. A young woman remembered the moments that changed her life.*

## A Girl, 1933

It was bitterly cold on this first Christmas day. My parents were fed up with hearing what presents I wanted to have. I cried, feeling worthless. At that moment, she came down the road. She had something charming about her. ´All alone?´ She didn't say anything else. No greeting, nothing. On this afternoon, I would have liked to give this woman a piece of my mind. My good breeding prevented it. ´I'm not alone at all, but I'd only be in the way at home right now. Therefore, I like to stroll around a little.´ She smiled. Then she stared at me. I felt myself caught. Her look struck me right in the soul. Distasteful. At that moment, I believed I was dealing with a veritable devil incarnate. She was trying to take hold of my soul, but I fought back. Thus, we stood for a while. She with her gaze that aimed deep into my innermost being and me with my fear. After what seemed half an eternity she stroked my head. I instantly ran off, didn't look back. She was, I reckoned, possessed by a demon, of that I was firmly convinced. Only a demon could cling to the souls of people. When I later came to know what had happened to her, I was not surprised. However, that changed nothing about the circumstances. The demon had to look for another body in which it could survive. Just not me, I thought with horror. It would be the end for my family, complete, relentless destruction. I was reassured when I did not notice any change in myself. Yes, I remained the naive little girl.

But the choice for the demon was vast! Willoughby had a few thousand inhabitants, every single one of them was now endangered. I didn't dare to raise the alarm. Who would have believed a twelve-year-old girl? Therefore, I kept the secret to myself. Only years later did I realize that I had been wrong. The young woman had fallen victim to an accident. I regretted my grotesque notions and allegations. How I had done her wrong! Standing at her grave I asked her for forgiveness. This young, beautiful woman! What might she have been thinking of me! She had looked into my soul, of that I am still convinced today. But she didn't have to battle with a demon inside herself. Today I am seeing the events from back then from a different angle. Sometimes a shiver runs over my back and I imagine that I bear the blame for her death. I had driven the poor woman into suicide with my wild, infantile fantasies. How can I cast off these thoughts that haunt me even into horrible nightmares?

*Now it is the doctor's turn, the grandfather of the man who harbored the man from Vienna. Studying his impressions was a special matter, given the personal connection to his grandson. The night was still young. He read with recurrent fascination.*

## The Doctor, 1933

I went home as if remote-controlled. I couldn't get the image of the deceased out of my head. She had lain there like a sleeper. I had become acquainted with her a few hours before, had had a short conversation. That had been enough to fall in love with her. This girl broke my heart. Her voice penetrated the darkest recesses of my soul. When I learned what had happened to her, I couldn't believe it. In my surgery, I am confronted daily with gravely ill people. And I'm always telling myself that I must not be personally involved if an individual is defeated by the disease. The girl was beyond help. While there were no externally discernible injuries visible, she was no longer breathing. I remembered the delicate handshake she had bestowed on me. A warm, gentle hand touched my clumsy paw for a split second. Now her hands were cold. She lay there like a dreamer. Back home I sat down by the window and stared outside. My wife and children were not at home. No further inspection was necessary. Dollars to doughnuts they were doing the honors at the Christmas Mass. I had no stomach for this whole religious stuff, not after what had happened during the last few hours. A young woman arrived in our small town, rested for a while at Mrs. Judd's pension, changed clothes and turned into a *"Girl in Blue"*. Why she was grazed by the train will remain a question that may never be solved, by whosoever. What had driven her into this situation? She charmed me, was a happy person, at least that was my impression. Was it a rash, impulsive decision that cost her life? So young and beautiful, a rose that faded far too early.

That night I could not get a wink of sleep. Her image was constantly present. I officially recorded her death. That is part of my duties as a doctor. How unjust life can be! Some scoundrels live a hundred years and more and this petite person breathes her last on a Christmas Eve in a city that should have been but a small stopover for her. I tossed and turned, stared at the ceiling and there I saw the girl, floating in her fine clothes. I must have dozed off for a moment, my wife wanted to calm me.

'Everything's fine!' she whispered. 'Go back to sleep, you just had a bad dream.' I was surprised that it was 9 am already. I didn't want to go back to sleep. No, I left it at that and shortly afterwards my wife and I were having breakfast. Soon our children would jump from their beds and ask us how long it would take until they could open their Christmas presents.

*A time leap to the year 1940. The narrator, this elderly quaint fellow, accomplished something exceptional. And thus, the man from Austria's capital city who was so keenly interested in the fate of the "Girl in Blue" turned night into day and dealt with the records of the woman, who in those days had been that girl who believed for a short while that she had dealt with a demon at that extraordinary meeting during the Christmas season of 1933.*

## The Girl as a Young Woman, 1940

Day after day I intended to confide in my boyfriend. It constricted my throat to bear this guilt. Richard sensed nothing of all this. He liked my otherness. He paid me compliments, he handed me a bouquet of flowers every week. But I couldn't find the courage to come clean. I persuaded myself I had to cope with this madness myself. The young woman had not been a lunatic; no demon had implanted itself in her. No, on the contrary, she enchanted people with her grace, her kindness, her joy of life. How could I be so stupid to misjudge her to such an extent? Now, years later, I had to pay the bill. Nightmares haunted me every night in which I am trying to save the *"Girl in Blue"* from certain death. She dies in my arms, my blouse is full of blood, she gasps, wants to say something. I cannot bear her eyes gaping wide open. Then I wake up soaked in sweat, Richard is sleeping quietly next to me and I am about to wake him. As usual I recoil from doing it, go to the bathroom and lock myself in until I have calmed down.

And yet I should be glad to have such an affectionate boyfriend. He isn't one of the rough guys who hits you when he feels like it. He is attentive, not only because of the flowers. I am fortunate to have him. Deep inside me the ´Unsaid´ is piling up, waiting to break free. I don't want to burden my parents with my fears, my female friends are too silly to understand me. There's only Richard left, Richard, Richard, Richard! What if I slipped him a letter? No, rubbish! What are we together for, in good times and bad! Yes, he proposed to me a few times, I refused him every time. Me, a bride! I have a human life on my conscience, how can I show up in church in a white bridal dress? The Good Lord will throw up his hands in horror in the face of my wedding. Oh, and in the most serious case I could only refuse, say no. Mom and dad, I'm sorry for what I've done. You have no idea how I am agonizing over this! Richard, I want to be a strong girl and not disappoint you, even though you know nothing of this. Outwardly I am diligent and support my father in the shop. He has confided in me that I could take over the bookshop in a few years' time. Me being a bookworm, I'd be a perfect successor. Yes, why ever not. And one day I will atone for my sins by telling about my nightmares in front of an assembled audience. All of Willoughby will know the score about the greatest criminal that ever lived in this small town. True, all depends on my strength of will. It will be easier to place my trust in Richard. As long as I don't, I will not be able to lead a happy life. A shadow will darken my life for all times, just because I am so ashamed of my thoughts which I could not tame many years ago.

*Even though tiredness made the European give a start sometimes, he wanted to devote himself to a contemporary witness whom he could not get out of his head. He could not pin down this man. Back in the days of Christmas 1933 he kept his eyes open with an effort and was ready to enter a house of God.*

## The Hobo, 1933

Well, I don't want to tempt Providence, but I have no other choice. The matter did seem weird to me. I was sitting in front of the church as usual waiting to get a few crumbs. The girl gave me a nod, then I lost sight of her. I didn't stir from my spot for half an hour and asked myself who the girl could be. I didn't know her, surely not. Whoever comes to Willoughby for a visit, especially on the 24th of December? Because she stayed in the church for an infinitely long time, in my opinion, I went in to check. She was quick to locate. She was kneeling, lost in a prayer. This girl, pretty as a picture! Had she been up to no good? Who's praying fervently if they have a clean slate? Sure, we're all sinners, that's a given. Depends what we have what we have to pay for. She was completely alone until I stepped up to her. I didn't want to startle her. She suppressed a low scream. Put her index finger on her lips. Yes, I kept quiet. Then she invited me with a nod to sit next to her. I took heart, one is a gentleman after all, right? She smiled at me, folded her hands and closed her eyes. For a while I was undecided how to get out of this situation again. And thus it happened that for the first time in my life, I folded my hands and looked around the church. It is a beautiful place still. Countless days I had been begging for alms in front of this church because I had hoped for the charity of the good Christians. But who was I? A crook, a person bent on conning money out of people. I never gave a thought to the faith that brings people closer to God. Doesn't even have to be a church, God is everywhere after all, not only within the tabernacle. I didn't know what was happening to me. Did I perhaps have visions of paradise on earth?

We stepped out of church together. She gave me a coin. I watched her go until she disappeared round a corner. She had prayed for nearly one and a half hours. That could be a heavenly sign. Had she maybe included all residents of Willoughby in her prayers? No, I no longer believed that she had done something evil, that she, like the rest of us, had burdened herself with guilt. But why had she washed up in Willoughby of all places? I brooded over her for a long time. Something had changed inside me, something unforeseen. A few hours later I heard about the accident. I cried for her. You can believe me, you who were not present: she is a part of my personal history that I will never forget. And I will never stop remembering her and wondering why she met her death. That is my purpose in life.

*As the man from Vienna stood at the window for a while to think about the records, he noticed how quiet it was all around. Willoughby seemed to have fallen into a deep slumber. He drank a little water and then looked at his watch. He wanted to find some sleep yet this night, but the young woman wouldn't let him go. She couldn't tear herself away from the "Girl in Blue"; her life in 1940 was unabatedly ruled by the unknown woman, however much she tried to lead an independent life.*

## The Girl as a Young Woman, 1940

A bookstore has some merit. For instance, if there are no customers in the shop, there's ample time to reflect. Sometimes it takes hours for anyone seeking reading material to stray in here. But I can't complain. I'm not a small child anymore even when there are moments when I feel taken back to my childhood. Then I see this young woman in front of me who had cast a spell over me in those days. Is there a spell upon me? Richards asks me every other day if I am ready for marriage, but nothing changes my refusal.

I read a lot to kill time. I have discovered *Alfred Adler*, the founder of 'Individual Psychology'. What's that stuff you're corrupting your head with, girl? Richard doesn't understand me, he just does not know the score. If I don't take him into my confidence I have to seek my salvation in another way. Individual psychology is quite suitable for this. I've read *'What Life Could Mean to You'* four times during the last months. And have partially understood it. It's probably the inferiority complex that causes me to torment myself. There can be no question of a superiority complex in my case, more likely it is Richard who is affected by this. The young woman could have helped me. She made me the person I am now. It is not her fault; I am entirely responsible for it myself. The nightmares won't let go of me. Usually Richard shakes me to free me from the claws of horror. He is imploring me to come clean with him. But this would only make things worse. He would no longer be interested in me. I already am afraid every day that he'll leave me. I don't want to have a baby, heaven forbid!

It has pleased me to make 'Individual Psychology' part of my life. Richard is teasing me about it nearly each day. Yes, I admit it; I am expecting help from the books. *Alfred Adler* is one thing. Basically, every book can give one's own life impulses, a new orientation. You precocious girl! Yes, Richard, don't I know. You don't like the fact that I read so much! But what else should I do? I can consider myself lucky to inherit a bookstore. So much spirit wafts from every nook and cranny! I am only at the start of a great journey, never mind how much Richard gripes. The latest nonsense is that he calls me emancipated. Whatever is that supposed to mean? I'm doing what I think is right. Maybe I am just emulating the young woman. In any case it's not complicated. Books broaden the perspective on the world. And I stick to honoring literature. It is just a pity not being able to get into direct contact with *Alfred Adler*. It would be wonderful to exchange a few words with him, to tell him about my suffering. He would understand me! Oh well, so I am condemned to lead this life. A life, the meaning of which is at least imaginable as a possibility through *Alfred Adler*. I just have to discover this meaning.

*The narrator gave no quarter for his protagonist. The European was very close to sleep, and yet he was condemned to take up the perspective of the doctor once more, who was devoted to the girl killed in the accident in an inexplicable love. Just one more time keeping his eyes open this night!*

## The Doctor, 1933

At first Britta reacted with a screaming fit. I humored her. Doesn't happen every day that the own husband tells of a dead woman who has turned his head. Then Britta was silent. She did not ask anything anymore, withdrew.

This is hell in my head. I don't know myself anymore. No, that's not quite true. I am getting to know myself anew, also learning who I am. No person is branded from the beginning as who he has to be. Neither am I. I travel in my own tracks, I see divergences. Suddenly a thought hits me that I instantly want to condemn: will Britta leave me? After all she knows now about my curious fascination with a deceased who has not even been buried! I have closed her eyes. They looked at me before, putting me in a state that nearly resembled ecstasy. I sensed the love that poured even from those dead eyes.

Is this possible, can this be? Someone who is dead becomes something intrinsic. She came to this small town to discover something. Did she find it? Is it even me she was searching for?

It's no use fooling myself. I told Britta just that, point-blank. This young woman has conquered my heart. Alive, she looked into my heart, dead into my soul. We belong together, are bound together by an eternal bond.

´Mister, I won't allow that we jeopardize our marriage over this!´ Britta is telling me this with tears in her eyes. ´You can swoon over this dead woman however much you like, the kids need a father, so be aware of your damned duty to care for your family!´ I give Britta a nod. My family is sacred to me!

´Santa Claus was here and has brought you something´ Britta calls in the direction of the children's room. A little later the children are standing in front of us in their pajamas. They are wide-eyed. I'm trying to stop my thoughts wandering, to share the children's joy. They are skipping around the room, never getting tired of looking at the presents. And they have painted two very beautiful drawings for Britta and me. Yes, I manage to unwind for a few hours, to let the pretty girl be dead and to pay attention to the living.

But two questions go round and round in my head on this first Christmas day as I watch the children playing with the small railway set: what will happen to the stranger? Will I have to do the coroner's inquest?

*The night had yielded to the day and the Austrian who had set forth to learn more about the history of the "Girl in Blue", finally obtains a name. Also, the identity of the girl our novel is focused on so elaborately will be revealed. The narrator has made a good job of it. Betake yourselves with him to the year 2013 again.*

### A European in Willoughby, 2013

´I'm still surprised what prompts an Austrian to concern himself with this story. And then you're taking it upon yourself to travel here, too.´

I have to admit having posed that question to myself already. Mr. Keanes is facing me over breakfast. To my own surprise I have slept very well after all the reading and I am thirsty for action.

´Oh well. We have known each other for a few years, right? I would never have expected to receive an answer from you. But then I smelled a rat. This accident wouldn't let go of me. A young woman makes a stop in Willoughby, rents a room at Mrs. Judd's, then transforms herself into the *"Girl in Blue"*, lingers a little in church, then greets half the population of Willoughby with extreme friendliness, which leaves a lasting impression on many people. And a few hours later she is hit by a train and meets her death. It was necessary to reconstruct this true story as accurately as possible. To find contemporary witnesses, maybe to discover something that would lift the mystery to a certain extent. To be present in Willoughby right now and not just to browse through diaries, notes, notebooks, police records and photo albums is something like the fulfilment of a dream. You, Mr. Keanes, have made this stay possible for me. For that I will be eternally grateful to you!´

My host smiled at me. ´Don't flatter me too much, Mr. Scherenschleifer! After all you're only at the very beginning of your adventure. Who knows what you'll be thinking of Willoughby, its residents and the *"Girl in Blue"* later.´

We finish our meal without haste. Ham with two eggs, a jam sandwich and a lot of coffee cheer me up. Mr. Keanes is a vet and his surgery is closed this morning. He doesn't want to let me go to the cemetery alone. His expert company is important to me, anyway. He knows the cemetery by heart, after all. His wife and kids wave us goodbye. We will be back in two hours at the latest.

The cemetery instantly exerts a magical pull on me. I only knew it from photos. Furthermore, I had tapped into the worldwide web, so I could pin down its location and geometric form. To stride through this cemetery fills my heart with joy. Sooner than anticipated we are standing in front of the grave of Josephine Klimczak. I am just in the middle of saying a silent prayer when I feel a blow on my right shoulder. I'm turning around, startled; an old woman is looking wide-eyed at me.

´Go away, go away, d'you hear?´ I'm looking to the side, where Mr. Keanes is standing.

´Don't worry, that's just Karen...Everything's all right, my dear´ he's talking to her tenderly. ´This is a friend from Vienna who's taken the long way upon himself to visit Josephine. Ain't that crazy?´ Karen's expression is changing. Where just now fear had been mirrored in her eyes, a smile is playing round her lips.

´Oh, well that's something. If only I knew who you are?´ She is slightly pressing her left index finger into the chest of Willoughby's vet. ´But Karen, you know right well. I'm Alfred Keanes, you've had your dog at my surgery for treatment several times by now.´ Karen is shaking her head. ´Not that you seem familiar to me. But if you say so, it'll be true.´ She is pushing herself between Mr. Keanes and myself. The three of us are standing in front of the grave of the "*Girl in Blue*". It is literally deadly silent, until Karen utters a faint scream.

´What is the matter, Karen?´ Mr. Keanes puts his hand soothingly on her shoulder.

´She is sad, very sad. Soon it will be eighty years since she has been hit by that stupid train. She cannot forget that. She has entreated me to send you away. You are unbidden visitors! Nearly every goddamned day spectators come who have learned of her fate. That makes her nervous. It won't make her come alive again. I am the only one whose visit she expects. Day by day. She can do without you, it only makes her angry.´ Karen makes no move to chase us away. She seems to have instantly forgotten what she has just said. ´I can give you homemade cookies. They are in my bag.´

She digs around in a monstrous-looking handbag and with a beaming face hands Mr. Keanes and me what she thinks are cookies. We thank her.

'Karen, I think it's about time that you went back. The warden is surely already worried about you.' She appears puzzled.

'I can't leave Josephine alone! That is against the rules and you know it!'

I offer my arm to Karen and she tucks her arm into mine. 'Oh, a real gentleman!' She presses a kiss on my cheek. We slowly begin to move. During our short walk Karen recounts numerous things. After we have taken her back to the retirement home, where she instantly takes a seat at a table in the dining room and gets her lunch served after a while, we make our way back home. Mrs. Keanes is waiting for us, an apron tied round her waist.

'I presume you have met Karen?' Alfred Keanes chuckles.

'You bet. And it surely wasn't the last meeting.' I feel like having completely arrived in Willoughby now.

# FIRST PROTOCOL

Yesterday a severe accident occurred in our small town. At a yet undefined time, certainly in the evening, a young girl, unknown in Willoughby, met a terrible death. She was hit by a train and then hurled into the forest, thus breaking her neck. Outwardly, she remained unharmed. The girl only had 90 cents and a train ticket to Corry, Pennsylvania, on her. No one can provide information on the girl, who apparently arrived in Willoughby by bus on Christmas Eve. As a Mrs. J. affirms, she offered the girl an accommodation for the duration of her stay. The girl had gone to church after having rested for a few hours. She wore a blue dress and blue shoes. This being interesting insofar that before she changed her clothes, she was wearing rather unassuming attire. Two citizens of Willoughby claim to have witnessed the circumstances of the accident in detail. Unfortunately, however, there are inconsistencies. One middle aged man put on record that the girl literally ran headlong into the train. He had had the impression that she was only waiting to throw herself towards the train. This would support a suicide theory. However, a woman close to 30 testified that she had noticed a shadow that had somehow taken influenced the accident. She could not specify who might have cast that shadow. A somewhat confused notion, but it is being verified presently. Whether suicide, murder or accident: the citizens of Willoughby are deeply shocked. Many people tell about a personal encounter with the girl. She had greeted them most kindly, wished them a Merry Christmas. A little small talk inevitably took place. No one speaks ill of the girl. She had been lovely, of radiant beauty, attractive, cheerful and with a sincere, all-embracing charisma. This raises the question of whether the severe incident is a crime or a sad occurrence, of which the precise course of events will never be solved. Up to now, almost everything is obscure. Certain is that the girl shall be buried in the cemetery of Willoughby.

*We may consider ourselves lucky to become ever more closely acquaintanced with the treasure trove of the researcher called Scherenschleifer. It is necessary to go back almost to the beginning of the story. The man from the bus slunk like a phantom through Willoughby to see the girl again. The accident had yet to happen at this point.*

## The Stranger, 1933

I couldn't get the girl out of my head. I awoke with a start, thought I heard her knocking on the door. I quickly got dressed and then opened the door. No girl to be seen. I tapped my brow. Was it all just imagination? I had met the girl in flesh and blood; there was no doubt about that. I had accompanied her from the bus to Mrs Judd's. If only I hadn't been such a coward and had invited her for a cup of hot chocolate! Now I was standing there dressed as if for an Antarctic expedition and kept rubbing my eyes. No, it couldn't be helped. I had to get some fresh air. Winter was taking a short break, or maybe it was just the cozy jacket. What if the girl vanished now and I wouldn't get to exchange another word with her? I would never forgive myself. Nothing remained to be done but to begin to search for her. Willoughby is not a major city; chances were quite good of meeting a pretty woman around 9 pm. Indeed a few ladies put in an appearance, but mine wasn't amongst them. I asked if they had seen 'my girl' but never got an answer. To hell with them!

I roamed every street, combed every side alley, even went along the cemetery. Then back again, the whole thing three times at least. I watched out for her like a maniac. Girl of my dreams, where are you? She could be everywhere and nowhere. Maybe she was asleep or she was long since on her way to another city. But there, only two houses behind Mrs. Judd's! Isn't that her? At my age, you get out of breath fast. Coughing and cursing I approached where I had imagined having seen the girl. No, it wasn't her. I'm such an idiot! She had moved on, was turning round a corner...How stupid of me that I had not called out. I didn't want to cause a stir, after all a lot gets interpreted the wrong way. I would not give up looking for her. For now though I did call it a day and headed for my little house. Huddled in front of the fireplace I brooded for half the night. I could have imagined anything but that my purpose in life would be searching for a girl that was unknown to me. I couldn't get it out of my head until sleep finally overpowered me, which granted me sweet dreams.

*The doctor's records were especially challenging for the narrator. I asked him what it is that attracts him to this character? He smiled at me and uttered a spell under his breath that I did not know. We set the clock anew, the doctor did not under any circumstances want to give up the connection to the girl he had been allowed to meet only for a few moments when she was still alive. Her death unabatedly gnawed at his soul...*

## The Doctor, 1933

Coming clean with my wife didn't suit me so well very soon. But I had had no other choice. How could I have kept my adoration for this unknown young lady permanently hidden? Britta didn't lecture me, she finally told me about the Christmas Mass which she had celebrated with our children in tow.

'You'll be glad to hear that your new love was topic number one! Yes, they all talked about her, and they spoke highly of her! A man reported that he had seen her lying dead. Allegedly he exchanged a few words with the doctor, meaning you. This man must be new to Willoughby; he had a very unkempt appearance. Words bubbled from his mouth like a waterfall. He had seen this girl alive in passing; she had greeted him kindly and beamed at him with beautiful eyes. Even as a corpse she had lost nothing of her grace. After mass, we stood together for a few minutes, the women gibbering like geese, the men gushing out hymns of praise about the lovely lady whose life had been over all of a sudden. No sign of any Christmas spirit, I can tell you!´ I did not fail to hear the acrimonious undertone that underlined my wife's last words. She was anything but pleased about the experience.

´Indeed, I can remember the slightly dishevelled man. I was just examining the body a little when he approached me.´

´She's a looker, isn't she, Mister? A real looker, that one!´ A curious thing to say in the face of the corpse lying in front of us. I asked the stranger not to disturb me during my examination. But he did not desist and kept pushing forward. ´You don't have to pretend with me, doctor! You're feeling like the rest of us who have a heart in their bodies. The lady has aroused your pleasure, just admit it!´ You can imagine, Britta, that I felt like struck by lightning. This obscure vagabond was voicing exactly what I had been thinking that very moment! I looked up quickly to give him a piece of my mind when I realized that he wasn't there anymore. Just gone, as if the earth had swallowed him up. He must have gone to Christmas Mass...´

My wife did not speak a single word again with me that day. She left me a written message that I picked up from the floor. She made it perfectly clear: You need not think I am a monster. Your love for a deceased has hurt me deeply, yet I do not want to endanger our marriage by a rash decision. Therefore, I am asking you to sleep in the guest room for now and in future. You can conduct your studies there and do not need to have consideration for my beauty sleep. We will remain a married couple if only for the children's sake. But you must expect nothing from me anymore, my love for you has cooled off and it will not be possible for you, whenever, to heat it up again. Your Britta.

I swore loudly, which almost never happens to me. I had only myself to blame for these new circumstances. I could not help myself, this girl had turned my head. I went to church on the same day. For a confirmed atheist like me, that's a rarity. Two or three old crones sat in a pew and gawped at me, surprised. I did not care. I sat down two rows behind the gossipers and prayed. Yes, I prayed! I sat there with folded hands and prayed for the salvation of this poor, dead girl!

´He should be ashamed of himself, ashamed! If he wanders in here at all, then he should go to confession straight away and not just fold his hands!´ One could not fail to hear it. I paused in my prayer, waiting for them to go.

´Bah, all of sudden he's pretending to be oh so pious and hasn't shown up a single time in church since his first son died!´

That was too much! I wanted to leap to my feet, bestow a cruel death upon the accomplished lady, then had a change of heart after all. Let them talk about whatever they wanted to! I did not care. I decided to go to church more often. Not to mass, under no circumstances, but for silent prayer only. Alas, all of a sudden, I began to accept God as a possibility. After the violent death of a girl, of all things! Isn't that completely crazy? After I had left the church I made a little detour across the cemetery. My little boy has been buried there for a few years. I had visited his grave three years ago last time. I did not have the heart to linger at this memorial. The girl may have flipped a switch in me. I cried, cried in remembrance of the boy whom an incurable disease had killed. I cried as I had never done before in my life. And later this day I once more entered the church to light two candles for my dear departed.

*Nearly nine years after the accident the former girl confided an incident to her diary by which everything should change. And this took place in times of war. We are looking over the shoulder of a young woman who was obviously willing to enter into more intimate relationships with books only. If we disregard the "Girl in Blue" who also seems to dominate her life.*

## The Girl as a Young Woman, 1942

Richard only knows one single topic: war! He doesn't understand that I am not interested in the political dimension. Yes, I am an apolitical person. What happened in Europe during the last few years has passed me by. With one exception, and that has to do with my bookshop. A few months ago, a book was ordered by a customer which has been available in its English translation for a short while only. Hitler has written it. I will never read this book, even if the customer has never collected it. He has never entered the shop again. Is he ashamed for his interest in this work? I don't mind being confronted with abysmal things. Every person has chasms, this Hitler has an abnormal one. The slaughter and killing is a consequence of the insanity that can have its place in a mind.

War plays a terrible game. The spawn of the devil has severely shaken the world. Richard does not want to hear this; he rather talks about Pearl Harbour. I am appalled by his words when he slings mud at the Japanese. He can't get over the fact that he wasn't declared fit for military service. His congenital heart defect makes it impossible for him to partake as a soldier in this war. I am still reading *Alfred Adler*, which is making Richard furious. 'You'll get square eyes from this! What's the point of all of it? The war will soon overrun the whole world and you're pondering the big questions of life...Moral integrity is gone nowadays anyway, what can you do about that?' Richard's significance in my life is beginning to wane. Who knows how long we will still endure each other?

And then he surprises me.

'I'm sure you can remember that girl that was hit by a train back then? Her name is still not known, for a time there was talk that she had fallen victim to an assault. A while ago I thought of the girl and remembered a situation which I had thought forgotten...'

Richard cannot guess that a cold shiver was running down my back. I would like to urge him to come clean with me. Instead I say, 'Ah yes, that girl...did you have anything to do with her?' I smile at him sardonically.

'What you're thinking again...she ran into me when I stepped out of the house. Was obviously in a hurry. Apologized a thousand times. She was somehow euphoric, wanted to get a present for her fiancé. I didn't inquire further; it was none of my business. She showed me a photograph. I cannot recall his face, time has blurred it. But you can take it from me: she would have done anything for this person...'

Oh, I was on the brink of revealing the secret. But I held back. Richard was amused about the story he might have dredged from his subconscious.

´What do you think?´ he asked with a broad grin.

´Weird that you would remember it now. It must be...wait...eight years ago, right? I have never made the acquaintance of that girl.´ Richard hesitates. ´Am I hearing correctly, dear? As far as I know, your parents were worried about you. You were quite besotted with this gal. She's supposed to have looked deeply into your soul.´

Has Richard known everything from the very beginning and has just waited for this moment? ´Did mom...´ He puts his hand on my arm.

´There's nothing bad about it. You liked her, you were fascinated. I could not completely elude her charisma, either. Probably no one could. There never has been a creature like her in all of Willoughby and there most likely will never be one again. I am just surprised that you won't admit your encounter. You will have your reasons, the question is just, which ones...´

I was taken by surprise. Henceforth I could save myself the whole secretiveness. The war is not the main topic for Richard anymore, instead the girl is! I cannot believe it.

´The truth is...this young woman has changed my life forever. She has predefined the direction. Sometimes I think that she talks through me, is a part of me. That is crazy but I just can't help it. I feel...´ No, I could not admit to the guilt weighing on me as well. It had to suffice that the young woman is no stranger to me.

From that day on the relationship between me and Richard is changing. He doesn't mention the war anymore; he doesn't mention the girl anymore. For the most time, he hangs around, has changed into a night owl. He has told me his story that connects him to the girl. Our relationship is ultimately endangered by this. Is that of any importance? Basically, she has always stood between us. I bury myself in my books, gossip with customers about this or that. Just to get rid of the thought of being a lost soul, because another has taken possession of it...

*During a few quiet moments Mr. Scherenschleifer spread out the material of the case of the "Girl in Blue" in front of himself. It was impossible for him to get even the tiniest distance at the scene of the event. Could anything be deduced from the witnesses' reports? To what extent could the explanations of the doctor's grandson aid him, whom he owed so much? And how much time should he allow himself, so he could at least match a few of the puzzle pieces better? The man from the bus remains a phantom.*

### The Stranger, 1933

I woke up. Dreams couldn't be that sweet. And then I heard her voice. This was not a dream any more, this was real. I had the feeling of having slept for many hours. A glance at the wall clock showed it was 11 pm. Christmas Mass starts in one hour. The girl had confused me. Were my senses thus paralyzed that I could not think straight anymore? I jumped out of bed, got dressed quickly. It had not even been two hours since I had been wandering around outside in search of the girl. Barely had I stepped outside the house that I noticed the turmoil. My neighbor crossed himself.

´A disaster has happened. A big disaster.´

I stepped up to him. ´What has happened, Mr. Schmidt?´

He whispered in a broken voice. ´The girl, she has departed this life. A disaster. A big disaster.´

A girl has died, but which girl? ´You're talking in riddles. Do you know more about it? Did you know the girl?´

Mr. Schmidt points to the heavens. ´No one ever saw her in Willoughby prior to the present day. She was a beauty, an angel from paradise. And then she ran into a train.´

With that my neighbour could only mean her, my girl! I had wanted to follow her tracks. Had she been afraid? Was that the reason she had sought out death?

A small cluster of people had formed around the site of the accident. There was little talk. I noticed a man clothed in rags who spouted incoherent stuff. Apart from that the silence was nearly insufferable. I was able to advance into the proximity of the deceased without problems. She lay there as if sleeping, dreaming. I ran off as fast as I could. This sight had deeply disturbed me. Never again would I exchange words with this young lady, never again look into her beautiful brown eyes, never again admire her smile, never again feel her joy of life as infectious. Life is never fair. I had to accept the girl's death. I went towards the church, like an automaton. I walked closer to the building. Like remote-controlled I finally sat down in a pew as far back as possible. I only took part in the festivities in a limited way. Defeatedly, I stared at the ground most of the time. All of sudden I imagined feeling a tender kiss on my cheek. I looked up, yes, that's her! She is not dead; it was all just a stupid dream. I have finally found her. But the very next moment she was gone. I looked around in all directions. Where had she gone to? I left the church right after communion hoping to see her again. Every shadow now seemed to have her silhouette. After a few minutes, the faithful and less faithful stepped out of church and congregated mainly in the courtyard. Should I ask about the girl? I stood a little apart; a cruel coldness seized my body. At that moment, I regretted not being dead myself.

*If protagonists of a novel are assigned names, identification with the characters becomes easier. And if relationships between the involved parties are established, then all of sudden even the narrator's magic spell makes sense. A few weeks after the accident the dust had settled a little. But the hobo who wore his heart on his sleeve wouldn't quit. And so, the story starts gaining momentum...*

## Will, the Hobo, 1934

I betook myself to my heels, even if they were somewhat worn. The police were surprised that I was interested in the case. It had long been filed. It was impossible to believe in anything but an accident or a suicide. I tried everything to prevail upon the criminal investigators not to get back to business as usual. After all a person had died! A girl that had cast a spell over all of Willoughby a few hours before her death! How was it possible to assume only an accident or a suicide? The police took a statement from me, that was all. This statement is now part of a file which shall never be dealt with again.

If the police don't do anything, that does not mean I will remain idle. Yes, I got cracking. Left my comfort zone. I incessantly asked the citizens of Willoughby if they could give me any relevant information. No response came back, absolutely nothing. Until I met this doctor. He had examined the deceased, had determined the cause of death. And he did not send me packing. With a tired look, he even invited me to eat with him at a roadhouse. I hadn't banqueted as well as that for ages! Oh, and the good wine to go with it!

'You're something else!' I show my benefactor respect and offer him my hand. 'My name is Will.'

'Will in Willoughby', he jokes and takes my hand. 'We can be on first name terms. I am Peter.'

We finished off two bottles of wine that afternoon and stuffed our bellies. During the whole time, we talked solely about this unknown girl. Peter showed me notes that he had taken.

'If you want, I can lend you the records. But you have to look after them very carefully. The matter is not without personal interest. Like you, I ask myself if that was just an accident that requires no further investigation. The girl ran into this train, what a tragedy! Maybe she was driven to put her life on the line. Or there's a secret that we cannot possibly know of. I also think that ultimately this is a criminal case. She broke her neck, death must have been instantaneous. There are no traces that would indicate a perpetrator who seized her and pushed her in front of the train. Could she just have waited for the train because she was yearning for death? It all doesn't make sense to me. Wasn't she so happy, so cheerful, turned a few men's heads quite all right, and made women jealous?'

'I am reluctant to interrupt you, but can't a motive for a crime be derived from these preconditions? A man harassed her and then, after he was refused, pushed her full of hate in front of the train? Or a woman got wind of the fact that her man had looked a little too deeply into her eyes, confronted the girl and then lost it because the smile did not vanish off the face of the beauty? It can't be denied that it might have been this way...´ I have to admit that I was very drunk at that time. But my mind was wide awake. Peter's words floated about in my head and let all kinds of theories arise that could possibly help the police to reopen the case anew. Peter stopped me with a wave of his hand.

´You can forget about that, Will! That's over and done with. Read through my records, and then we can talk further on occasion. And here's a little cash, you should get your hair cut sometime!´

Still on the same evening I buried my nose in Peter's notes. They made it clear to me that there was one person who did not close the dead girl's case thoughtlessly. His descriptions of other deceased persons who had died under mysterious circumstances pursued me right into my dreams. No, it wasn't about women who were hit by a train. But there a man was struck to death by a gravestone, a child fell out of a window, a woman took an unlucky fall. In all three cases, it was unclear whether they were just accidents. Peter had voiced his concerns to the police. Today the files have fallen prey to the shredder. The notion that the cases are unsolved exists only in Peter's head. I can only agree with him. It is easy to see what has occurred the way it has most likely happened. But there is always an element of uncertainty whether everything actually has been like that. I was very glad to have found a person who had a similar interest in the case like myself. I had snapped at Peter still at the site of the accident at the time. I was sure the whole time that we spent with each other that he knew whom he confronted. A noble person, this Peter! Not at all resentful and a critical contemporary. Who knows, maybe we'll even become friends. And I will spend the money on a visit to the barber shop; I don't want to cheat him on that. He will be surprised whose face is hiding behind the growth.

*When the narrator enters the stage, literature and life coalesce. He means to create a last great work. And was ready to do anything, even if that entailed bitter agony. Thus, he left his characters for a few lines and put the focus on himself.*

## The Narrator, 2013

Slowly, time is running out on me. I started in my early twenties. The manuscript was sent back to me after a few months. During the next years I often received the same answer from publishers: ´Unfortunately your manuscript does not fit into our product range. We regret having to send this letter of refusal, but wish you all the best in the future!´ And has this future arrived now, more than 60 years later? I have never ceased in my endeavor to create something special. I have always been aware of my skill of expressing myself well in writing. It took 30 years till the first publication, a small volume of poetry. It was printed in an edition of 300 copies. I had to pay a subsidy. Rather few were sold. Only after six years 50 books had passed over the counters. Internet did not exist back then. The 1970ies had not been waiting for poems dedicated to nature. A lot of trash was produced all around which has increased distinctly nowadays. I am appalled at how much idiocy the bookstores are offering. Most likely every other who is capable of writing thinks he is an author. But there they have another think coming. Anyone who's writing and publishing their literature has a great responsibility. It's not enough to just write down anything. The level is falling with the bestseller lists. Sometimes there's a gem amongst them that is much sought-after for inexplicable reasons. That's where marketing is apparently working really well.

Alfred likes to listen to me. He seldom says anything himself. I am something of a unique specimen for him, a literary crossover. I talk about my passion for literature. That's how it has started after all. Only he who has a passion for literature might want to contribute something himself one day. Reading and writing is more than deciphering and retracing of letters. It all happens in the mind. Fantasy plays wild games, imagination is in demand. Each sentence can cause its own association. I can see the scenario in my mind's eye when I read something. If I write something, I immerse myself in the world of those people whose fates I describe. My so far only novel followed not ten years after my volume of poetry. Again, I indulged in descriptions of nature; I let a flower muse about her world. A publishing company took pity on me and I did not even have to pay anything for it. The novel met with no success. That's how the years passed. Alfred drinks coffee at my place every second day.

´At 86 I finally want to realize the project of my life. I must look ahead. Who knows how long I'll be in full command of my mental and bodily faculties. Therefore, I am doing everything to make progress. I won't take any interfering. My son is asking me why I am doing this to myself. I should enjoy my life. He of all people thinks he knows what's good for me! He himself has no time for anything. He's either hanging around in his office where he's organizing projects or he's flying halfway around the world to land some contracts. I have no idea what his actual job is. The main point is he wants to lecture me! What do you say to that Alfred? You have to have an opinion on that?´

It goes on in this vein for almost two hours. Alfred mostly shrugs his shoulders. He never phrases more than one or two sentences.

´Yes, that's good, that's very good. You're the best!´

His contributions are pretty much like that. He is demented, the good fellow. I look after him, go shopping with him, knock on his door every morning. He has no one else after all. He doesn't want to move to a care home, there's only murder and manslaughter there. They might as well bury him right away. His daughter doesn't care for him. A geriatric nurse only comes once a day and does the bare necessities. We elderly have to get organized ourselves and support each other if the young ones rather pursue their careers which robs them of their last strength. I am saying this frankly. Georg, that's my son, has wanted to commit me to a care home several times before. You will thrive there, he said. Yeah, sure, my boy, dream on! I remained steadfast and am not just pretending to be independent! I can get nearly everything done myself, even cooking, doing the washing-up and vacuum cleaning. For the rough stuff, help arrives once a week in the form of a pretty young woman from abroad. She has cleaned the windows, washed the curtains and hung them, even cut my toenails. Yes, that also has to be done. She has talent for this and does get pretty good money for it.

What can writing accomplish? Can the world be set on fire by a novel? I once believed in that, but that was a delusion.

Writing can still create something great: a world aside the known, a world of inner strengths, a world behind the curtain! The visible and the invisible are at home in the very same world. I prefer the examination of the invisible. This has not changed after more than 65 years of writing. Now I am working on this monster project and asking myself: will I get to an end? Is it not far too illogical whatever is strung together in events and perceptions? But isn't writing the end of logic? Does everything have to be perfectly clear? Failure is always a possibility. This time it would break my heart if I failed. I have invested too much. I have really delved into the story. I don't want to think in the end that I have failed again. I don't even know what I am aiming at. Can something like the ultimate literary work exist? After that, nothing follows, the inner struggle for the one's life work comes to an end. But does that insight ever happen? Can an author be satisfied and lie down peacefully to die? I don't want to do my son this favor so quickly, nor anybody else. I owe that to myself. I am drawing on my life experience, many sad, terrible years and many nice years that I was allowed to spend with my wonderful wife. Her death pushed me down a deep hole. Five long years I just withdrew into myself, did not want to live anymore. I lost weight, but all of a sudden, I found a new lease of life. Alfred is to blame for that. He advised me to write a novel that is about a special woman. Well, I don't know if it will really be a novel, and the story is not about my wife. But these women, whose appearance evokes delight and joy, exist. I want to make this the subject of my story somehow. By this I will indirectly erect a memorial in my wife's honor, because she had exactly that effect for me, she turned my head. Alfred saved my life. We shall remain friends until one of our hearts stops beating.

*After the creative break, the old man whom I selected as narrator of this story concentrated on his craft again. He once more described the 21-year-old bookseller and her involvement with the girl who is by this time known to us as Josephine Klimczak. We find ourselves once more in times of war.*

## The Girl as a Young Woman, 1942

Am I finally mad? In the sense of strayed off course, away from my roots? I am bored at the bookstore most of the time. In order that it doesn't get too dull, I reach for a book repeatedly and read a few lines. From fear of getting caught reading by a customer if they enter the bookstore, I keep the book open on the counter and my eyes constantly on the door. But once, I lose control. The she forms in front of me, floats from the pages. I look at her, my heart pounding wildly.

'This can't be, this cannot possibly be! Is it really you, you who has destined my life for years?' She does not speak, just looks at me. She smiles, I know that smile. It is the smile of our first and last encounter.

'I have disparaged you' I say ruefully. 'I was a girl without decency. I believed you were a demon. When I heard of your death, I instantly felt responsible. There was no escape! Year after year I attempted to redeem my terrible offense before God. A thousand times have I asked your forgiveness...finally I can look you in the eyes again! May my guilt thus be...´

´Hello?´ I awake from a dream. I'm standing there like a statue.

´Are you feeling unwell, should I call a doctor?´

I shake my head. ´I must have dozed off for a moment. Pardon me, Miss Leandros.´

She is my most loyal customer. She buys at least one book every week. Now and then we discuss her reading matter.

´Let me have a look´ she says, obviously concerned for myself. She throws a glance into the book that granted me a contact with the girl. ´The Interpretation of Dreams, Sigmund Freud! Isn't that old hat already? Do you believe in that, my dear?´

I sit down on a wooden chair for a moment, Miss Leandros brings me a glass of water.

´You know´ I start. ´I am interested in those parts of ourselves which we don't know. The unconscious rules our whole life. We suppress all sorts of things which in good time surface in our dreams.´ My favorite customer does not object. She deliberates a long time before she answers.´ Don't overdo it, promise me that! First Alfred Adler, then Sigmund Freud, what next? You're not doing yourself any favors!´ She is probably even right. She waits until I get up from the chair and walk behind the counter. Then she browses for a good half-hour.

´You've put me off my stride. I haven't found anything. Will you get in something new anytime soon?´ I can answer in the affirmative. I like that she worries about me. She may be the only person who takes me seriously.

And if it hasn't been a dream? I saw her so clearly before me! Before heading to bed in the evening, I pray for her salvation. I open the bible which drives Richard mad. He is up to something, scares me. He cannot see anything positive in my quest for meaning. Silence rules between us. The war lasts longer than we thought. It is time that the horrors come to an end. I suffer with the people war has stacked the deck against. Richard listens to the radio every day, but we do not discuss the war reports. The unknown girl has overshadowed our relationship. Richard is not the man of my life; that is no secret by now. He does not want to understand me, makes me unhappy. What can be thought of a man who doesn't enrich my life, but makes it poorer? I do not pray for him nor for a revitalization of our partnership. He only has himself to blame for this. Maybe his erstwhile marriage proposals have demoralized him. But this reaction wasn't to be expected. Before falling asleep I think of the girl like I do every night. Praying for her and thinking of her, so that this wound in my life will sometime be fully healed. It is necessary to believe in miracles.

*Mr. Scherenschleifer, the man from Vienna, felt comfortable in Willoughby almost 80 years to the day after the accident. He knew the records that had been leaked to him almost by heart and yet could not make head or tail of it. He was grateful for every howsoever small clue that might bring light into the darkness. And he yearned to personally meet a contemporary witness. This innermost wish blazed in him like a small fire.*

### A European in Willoughby, 2013

All that legwork. I almost wish I was back in Vienna. During the last days I have asked myself over and over again what I actually want to achieve here, what I am looking for? Willoughby is a completely distinct universe. It is hard to strike up a conversation with people. My English isn't the best either. My walks are never directed at a specific target. Alfred is a fine chap. He is trying to motivate me not to give in. He believes that my odyssey will be brought to a favorable conclusion. Time is flowing, it is like a run in a hamster wheel. Encounters result in small talk. Questions are never answered. It was probably too long ago. Will I have to leave without having accomplished anything? What did I expect?

The philosopher's stone? Ultimate knowledge? I imagined I would be able to uncover a secret. By reading the records and looking at the photos I am not progressing even an inch. Everything remains in darkness. I was so fascinated by this story; it is what transported me to this nice little town. At that I am seized by a shiver of happiness: I am in Willoughby, talking to people, having a good time, living for the moment. Living in the present in Willoughby!

Japanese are taking pictures at the grave. I am used to this from my hometown where the graves of honor on the ´Zentralfriedhof´ are sought-after photo subjects. Johann Strauß, Beethoven, Johann Strauß's father, Schubert. Hardly anyone finds their way to Salieri, who evidentially had been a good friend and an admirer of Mozart but never ever his murderer. I step closer to a young lady who asks me to take a picture of her and her friend. Then we talk about the "*Girl in Blue*". Yes, they have come here because of this girl. It has been a long journey from Tokyo. But they are satisfied. After all they are cemetery tourists. In any city they get to know for the first time, they always seek out the cemetery as their primary destination. Oh yes, ´Wien, Wien, nur Du allein!´ The pretty Japanese sings a hymn on Vienna in front of the grave of the "*Girl in Blue*". That is quite crazy. We talk for a while yet about commonplaces. I get my picture taken too. One picture shows me flanked by both Japanese women. Less than five minutes later, they move on. People from faraway countries are looking at the grave, some are praying. I am smiling to myself. My expectations have finally burst like a bubble. ´Go away, away!´ Karen rolls her eyes, spits on the ground. ´Lowlifes, stupid lowlifes! It's my turn, it's my turn every day!´

She takes my hand. Karen has not forgotten me. ´Don't get involved with these women, they are witches. They just mean to harm Josephine. Do you know what curses these stupid, stupid people are uttering? I don't want to insult you by taking those words into my mouth. Be so kind and push back these people. I want to talk to Josephine.´

Five, six people make way. Karen stands in front of the plot with me. She mumbles to herself. For a while she is transfixed.

´Where has she gone to? Where are the others?´

She rubs her eyes, looks around. ´I am sorry, I am dreaming with open eyes. Did you see her yesterday? Or do you want to have lunch? Breakfast time is over, isn't it?´ I calm down Karen who is trembling all over. She clings to me, plucking at my sleeve.

´Accompany me, young man!´

Arriving at the retirement home we sit down at a window table in the dining room. Flowers are wilting in a vase.

´Listen, you have to promise me to come to Christmas Mass! Josephine will thank you for it!´

I give her a nod. ´With pleasure!´

Originally, I had planned to be home for Christmas. Wife and child, my small family. I left them behind, but I don't miss them. Is this adventure in Willoughby maybe just an escape into certainty?

´You're spot on. I've watched you! It was time for you to come. So many years. You are the one Josephine loved. It's you, for sure!´

I try holding back my tears but don't succeed. Karen puts her arm around me. 'All right, my boy, it's all right!' I would have loved to have been born here, to have looked into this girl's eyes with rapture! Would it then have been possible to prevent the accident? People didn't know what was happening to them. They saw it as a gift to have met the girl. Maybe their concern was just catching a glimpse of the secret that surrounded Josephine. Maybe she was waiting for a declaration of love? She sympathized with every person she met. But did that lead to mirroring of image? The answers might have been so disappointing, so devastating, that she decided to take her life. Or am I just fantasizing?

'You are thinking of her; don't think I wouldn't notice that. We all think of her! Only no one admits it! They think of her day and night. Don't leave me alone! I will be here. Don't leave me alone!'

Before going to bed I tell Alfred about my tears.

'There will be a reason, my friend! Yes, you are called upon to accompany Karen to Christmas Mass. It will be an honor for my family to celebrate the holidays with you. You have been something like part of this family for years. Today I'll show you some records that have fallen into my hands only a few months ago. That might possibly help you to delve just a little more into the story behind the story...'

That night I am lying awake for a long time. It's just two days until Christmas. My wife screamed at me on the phone. She cursed me to hell and back. I didn't need to come back home at all, anyway it wasn't my home any more. She had always stood by me, but that was over now once and for all. My obsession had long ago taken on pathological traits. I should go see a psychiatrist. Whether our relationship could be salvaged was entirely up to me. My mind is completely made up: my wife can scream and clamor as much as she likes, she won't lay down any rules for me. Under no circumstances! It is not just my intention, it is my deepest innermost wish to spend Christmas in Willoughby.

# Farewell

*The role of the undertaker is of the utmost importance in the event of death. Mr. McMahon will accompany us now in our search for enlightenment of the circumstances that led to the death of the "Girl in Blue", by way of his diary entries, which he has each provided with an exact date.*

### 1933/12/25, Diary of the Mortician

Finally, I have some peace. The last hours have brought me close to breaking point. I still can't quite believe all that has happened. I have never kept a diary all my life, and in my old days I now take the pen and keep records. But I can't help myself. What has happened: yesterday I was preparing for the walk to Christmas Mass together with my family. We were all dressed up formally, I was joking that at this time surely no customer would be knocking on my door. I was wrong. A young man nearly fell in my house with the door, had to come up for air first. 'You have to come with me, Mr. McMahon! Something terrible has happened!' It didn't take me long to catch on that a person had died. As an undertaker it is my profession to spring into action then. In this case it was different, as I was soon to find out. I looked at the clock on the wall; it was half an hour before midnight. There is a woodlot in close vicinity to the railroad embankment. A cluster of people had formed there. It took me a while to fight my way towards the deceased. Peter shook my hand. ´We cannot leave her lying here all night, I'm sure you understand that, James!´

He had already determined the cause of death. Externally nothing could be observed about the girl. She seemed to sleep, looked like an angel. I noticed wildly gesticulating people, a woman yelled, and then ran away. Christmas Mass was the last thing on my mind. Since I have been living in Willoughby, I have never missed Christmas Mass. This time there was no other option: I stayed at the scene of the event. The distance to the funeral parlor was only a short one. But we still used a fitting vehicle for the transport. Around two am I delivered the unknown deceased to the cooling room.

Just five hours later I got up again, indulged in a small breakfast and dedicated myself to the girl. Before eight o'clock, Peter already showed up. ´Everything all right with you?´ he asked me with tired eyes. ´You've examined her. What have you found?´

I told him of my preliminary findings which he could largely confirm.

´The question is whether it was an accident or maybe a murder or suicide after all?´

I was surprised about the interest of Willoughby's doctor.

'As far as I can see, it can only have been an accident. The girl was hit by the train, broke her neck either right away or in consequence of the hard fall. What's giving you the idea that it could be murder or suicide?'

'A witness claims he saw a shadow in immediate proximity to the girl. Maybe she was even pushed in front of the train? And it might just as well have been that the stranger waited one, maybe two hours for the arrival of the train because she planned to take her life. After all no one saw her for hours, until immediately before the accident. I myself met her in person a few hours prior to her death. And...' Peter faltered.

'And?' I encouraged him to continue his narrative.

'And then I fell in love with her...Yes, that's how it was, so help me God!'

Meanwhile several citizens of Willoughby had gathered who wanted to pay their last respects to the girl. The news of the fatality had already gotten around.

'Wait! I have to prepare the deceased a little yet, wanted to start with it in the next few minutes...'

The few people left without having achieved anything.

'As you can see, I have work to do, Peter! And concerning your infatuation: that has blown off now, hasn't it?' He shook his head.

'No, on the contrary, I love her with all my heart!'

In the afternoon, the girl was visited by many people. At that time this was already possible, I had prepared her accordingly. Some lingered half an hour at her side, others not even two minutes. I was asked questions that I could answer only partially.

She will be buried, won't she, Mr. McMahon! You will arrange for a nice funeral!´

The chairwoman of the charity whispered to me in the face of death. ´We will start an appeal for donations! The poor woman deserves a dignified funeral. And you will do your best, you have to promise me that!´

I had not planned not to bury the unknown deceased. It is my duty after all to get the dead below the ground. Of course, this case is special. There are no bereaved who could pay for the funeral. The girl had no identification, no clue to her identity on her. One can already read in the papers what has happened in Willoughby. Who knows, maybe a close relative who misses her will come forward. Regardless, I get back to work. It is necessary to prepare everything so a fine funeral can take place. Anyone who has suggestions for the style of the ceremony can contact me directly. My wife lets me work in peace. I have retired to the study so I can think. Now I'm closing this diary for today. Maybe this is the beginning of a longer journey after all. I would never have considered ever writing down my thoughts. Now I feel a need to.

*The undertaker's diary had to be discovered anew by Mr Scherenschleifer. It was another matter with the records of the young woman which have thus far accompanied us into the years of WWII. He kept re-reading one of her favourite passages, because it showed the bookworm in a special light. The little girl of old had matured into a confident lady.*

## The Girl as a Young Woman, 1945

The war is almost over. Hitler is supposed to have killed himself. And it's over with Richard, too. He once more gave me a sermon. As if he knew my dos and don'ts. ´You can't just always hide behind your books! Life is waiting there, outside! I am waiting outside!´ He tried to talk me around, point-blank proposed to me again. Then, a few days ago, the ultimate end. He was watching me making my diary entries.

´Not just reading, now you're even writing! Wanting to be writer, eh?´ That was cruel. He wanted to take away my notes, made fun of me. I could not take that. ´You know what you are, Richard? A narcissistic asshole, exactly! You don't give me credit for anything, you mock me. And what about yourself? You're unfit for service, work for your daddy and cry if I give you the cold shoulder. Have you ever considered how I feel? I don't need you, you can move out right away, I'm not stopping you! The apartment belongs to my parents anyway, you were always just a guest here!´

At first, I thought he wanted to object as he had usually done before. But this time he screamed, as if I had doused him with gasoline from head to toe.

´You ungrateful bitch! I would have done anything for you, anything! You know that damn well. It's not my fault that I'm not fit for service! I'm going to knock the nonsense out of you yet…´

He would probably have killed me, but a knock on the door saved me. My brother stood there and looked into Richard's reddened eyes.

´Fuck off!´

He had heard everything. Richard didn't utter a single word and left.

I am not afraid that he might lie in wait for me. I ask myself how I could stand to be with him for several years. Was it pity? He was a rejected son, deep down a lonely boy who never grew up. To sling mud at my literary ambitions was a way for him to conceal his own defeats. He isn't capable of anything, anything at all. And maybe the story about the girl and her bridegroom is not even true? Yes, he can have made it all up to break through my reserve! I overcame my inhibitions and set foot in the cemetery for the first time in years. I had not been there since the funeral. I did not find the grave right away. When I stood in front of it, I cried my eyes out. I talked to her, to the girl. Who might she have been, the young woman, what did she want in Willoughby? Did she fall prey to a perfidious crime? Or did she lose her love of life and throw herself in front of a train because of that? Or if it was just an accident, some amalgamation of coincidences, that lead to her death? She did not answer. I did not even notice that it had grown dark. A hand took mine. It was Carl, my brother.

'You will catch a cold here, sis!'

He invited me over to his place. We dined together, laughed and talked about this and that.

'We were kids, but still we sensed that something special was happening. This young woman had looked into our hearts! She knew how we were doing. She was acquaintanced with us all, Willoughby wasn't unfamiliar to her. Maybe she had lived here before, moved away and no one could remember her any more. She greeted me and it sent a cold shiver down my back! This girl had magical powers. And I did not have the heart to admire her one more time…'

Carl held my hand the whole time.

'I sneaked into James McMahon's with a few adults. He only discovered me late. I could gaze more than once on this beauty. She wore this glorious blue dress, these cute little blue shoes. And a white blouse. 'Boy, this is not for the likes of you' he said with a little mischief in his voice. 'You will see plenty dead people soon enough in your life.'

But I did not want to go and he did not force me to leave the room. I was a child and the *"Girl in Blue"* was the first deceased that I paid my respects to. That gave my life a new direction. I asked myself how it would be if I had to die soon. I had never thought about death before, I was only barely eight years old. I'm not afraid of death. The girl stilled my fear. She lay there so peacefully. She is there now, too, somewhere in another world, in a world where pure love reigns. And we will end up there when our time has run out.´

Almost twelve years have passed since the accident. Not a day goes by when I don't think about the girl. Carl is just the same. And it took him a long time until he could tell me that he had seen the deceased. He couldn't tell anyone back then, thought our parents would punish him for it. And he didn't want to scare his big sister. He is so considerate, the darling.

*He still remained completely in the dark. He chased after the illusion that the girl might still be alive. But he endeavored to produce new relations. Thus, he turned towards the hobo. This meeting can only have taken place a few days after her death, when she was laid out at the funeral parlor of Mr. McMahon.*

### The Stranger, 1933

My journey led me all across the city. I looked around again and again. She is supposed to be dead, I asked myself. I have seen the mortal remains. But that wasn't her, I couldn't believe that.

He was sitting on the curb, eating something. I sat down next to him.

´May I ask you something?´

The not exactly smartly dressed young man hinted a punch at my solar plexus. ´Say it plain, if you please. I've got time, plenty of time!´ He scared me. His eyes flickered madly. Then I finally got past my fear.

´I doubt that this girl is dead. I met her at Christmas Mass. I've been looking for her.´

How monstrous was the laughter of this bear! He held his belly, slapped his thighs.

'Are you comfortable, brother? Buckled up? The girl's already lying over there at Mr. McMahon's, the mortician. The papers are reporting nationwide about the events in our damned town. Yes, finally something happened that's worth reporting. It's all over town: the girl is dead, there's no doubt about it. The question is just how it could have come about. I've been racking my brain about it since the day before yesterday. We've all watched her, no one is stone cold and doesn't weep tears over her pointless demise. She did not plunge into a canyon, wasn't shot dead by a crazed husband, didn't stumble headlong into a train. That would be completely insane! There must be more behind it, if you ask me about her. Although I can't get her out of my head anyway. She will have turned almost every local's head. The fat's in the fire, now we regret not having made her acquaintance sooner.'

For a few minutes we just sat there, he continued to eat, now and then spitting on the ground.

'I have this theory of mine', he suddenly said after a while and stared at me as if I was the devil himself.

'She took her life, because she had no other choice. Why was she so friendly to all of us, went out of her way with niceties? Probably just because she knew the writing was on the wall! She was aware that this was her last day on earth. She said goodbye to the world by wishing every person she met a Merry Christmas from her heart. She came to Willoughby to put an end to her life. That was nicely planned. She waited for the train, didn't hesitate one second. Then it was finally over. This sad life, just steeped in dark shadows...'

I mulled this over.

'But if all of this isn't true, because she is still alive?'

This wild man got up, held out his clenched fist against me.

'This man who is responsible for the death of this girl, I'll gladly dispatch into the happy hunting grounds, I can tell you that! I'll not rest until I know why it happened. There are only crude theories in the papers, the truth is known to the girl alone. I, however, am called upon to investigate this cruel death!'

I felt both warm and cold all over. I wanted to run away, wrap myself into a warm blanket and sleep, sleep, sleep…

'Stay here, man! First you dare disturb me during my only meal of the day, then you just want to vanish…sit down again, stranger! I don't know you, who knows, maybe you have something to do with her death and want to ease your conscience? Don't worry, I didn't mean it like that earlier. I won't kill you if you have confessed to me that you have driven the girl to her death! So, what's the matter, cat got your tongue?'

I just manage a croak.

'Li..listen, what you're implying is outrageous. I became acquainted with the girl. It seems to me as if that has been years ago. We sat on the bus and the way she moved impressed me. She was a real lady, beautiful and smart! I wished her eternal life! You don't even know…'

He smiled at me, patted me on the shoulder.

'I'm sorry, bro, sometimes I blow my top. I act up like that quite often. The one who's responsible for the deed hangs around Willoughby and isn't sure himself if she's dead. That can't be, right? Whoever is the culprit will have left town long ago. The perpetrator returning to the scene of the crime, that's nonsense! Anyone who's right in the head hightails it! So, I'm not suspecting you, sorry for upsetting you so much. You probably believed for a moment there you yourself were the culprit! You know what, I'll invite you for a drink. I've scraped together a little money ...´

I decline this offer with thanks. As far as I remember I have nothing to do with the death of this fair creature. I feel haunted by the girl, any time she can jump in front of me and cock a snook at me. But I won't let her fool me. Therefore, I once more resume my search, so she can't surprise me. I walk, walk, accompanied by the stars, along the never-ending road, at the end of which she might yet lie in wait for me...

## 1933/12/26, Diary of the Mortician

The matter has heated up. More and more people are paying their respects to the girl. Tears are flowing. Men, women and children are shattered. To give everyone the opportunity to say farewell I have posted my assistant at the entrance of the institute. He is sending the people into the chapel of rest one by one. More than three or four people shouldn't linger there at the same time. The girl is ready to be interred. There are incoming donations. The chairwoman of the charity told me beaming with joy that enough money has accrued.

´I insist that you use this money for your fosterlings. I don't want to touch the money you collected for the funeral.´

The woman bursts into tears.

´You are such a good person, Mr. McMahon! We have decided to get a special inscription made. The dead girl shall not go unnoticed. We owe her that. I speak in the name of the citizens of Willoughby!´ I squeezed her hand. ´A splendid idea! But as I said: don't worry about the funeral. I will do that voluntarily.´

I racked my brain last night how the fate of the girl is to be evaluated. Yes, I have also made her acquaintance. It is no use denying it. I just don't want to shout it from the rooftops. This creature was of an enchanting beauty, seemed to have descended from some star down to earth. Everyone is talking about her. I hear people whisper who look upon her mortal remains. Not a single derogatory word is spoken. Indeed, was she a saint? Peter's world has collapsed on him. He has unburdened his heart to me today. He cannot sleep, he cannot eat. At the moment he is useless as a doctor. ´It can't go on like this! You're a family man, you have duties!´

He almost shouts it out. ´My wife knows. I confessed it to her. She hasn't looked at me since. We don't sleep in the same bed anymore. The children are catching on that something isn't right, but they don't say anything.´ Peter is in danger of sinking more and more into an abyss where the girl is waiting for him. I call upon his common sense. ´There is no rational explanation for this. Maybe we are all just dazzled by her appearance.´ How shall I advise a good friend who has gotten himself into such a situation? He runs to the chapel every few minutes, remaining there for a while. I cannot send him away, that might be the end of him. ´I love this girl so much! She lives deep in my soul, to me she isn't dead!´

The day before yesterday something happened in Willoughby which will go down in history. Even in decades, centuries, one will know of it. There are events that will remain deeply engraved in our memories. Which leaves no one indifferent. Who was this girl? She will have relatives, mother, father, siblings, uncle, aunt, whoever. No one has gotten in touch about the calls in the papers. She remains unknown. I am writing all this with a heavy heart. My wife can come in any time and fetch me away from here.

I have returned after an interruption. My records for today aren't finished yet. I have offered Peter that he can get accommodation with us for a while. Our house is big enough. He can make himself at home in one of the guest rooms. Now he spends half the night with her. He wants to be near her. We are very concerned. Where shall this lead to? I get up in the middle of the night to check on him. Peter is sitting there with moist eyes and is holding the girl's hand.

'It's all right, my friend! Go to bed, sleep for a few hours. Tomorrow's yet another day.'

'It's ok', he says in a tearful voice. 'I'll just keep sitting here for a few more minutes.'

It is as if this great physician is just a shadow of his former self. The vital spirits seem to have deserted him. Any solace fails. He is distraught, babbles words which I do not comprehend. I must find sleep myself. My little records do me good. I am calm and concentrated now. The next days will be demanding. The funeral is imminent. Tomorrow Fred will craft a coffin. He's my best man for the job. I am struggling for words to describe what happened. All of Willoughby is under the spell of an unknown girl. There is just a single topic of conversation. Are we all condemned to be ruled by this event? Why not make the effort to try and get back to business as usual? The girl is dead, a terrible accident has pulled her down into the realm of death. My task as mortician is to inter the deceased with dignity. One of my best friends would like to put the dead one into a glass coffin so he can look at her every day until the end of his days. A doctor talks nonsense, negates the process of decay of a dead body. My head is full of thoughts. But I am tired, will write down just this sentence and go back to bed afterwards.

*Will was becoming a key figure. And furthermore, it was necessary for the narrator to give the other characters more clear-cut contours. Especially Mr. Scherenschleifer, who devoured the notes that had been newly handed to him in a minimum of time, took delight in this. And part of these records circulated a few days after the death of the "Girl in Blue", as we will soon learn.*

### Will, the Hobo, 1933

How glad I am to stretch my tired legs here. The landlord asks me every few minutes if there's anything else he can get me. But I have everything I need. A notepad and a pen. It's cold outside, I would catch my death out there. A few hours ago, a man yelled at me.

´Look here, you scum! Why are you fouling up the surroundings like that with your stench? Beat it or I'll kick your ass!´

I was on the verge of punching that guy right in the face. Then I thought better of it.

´What's gotten into you, if I may ask? Does my attire displease you, or is my perfume unpleasant to you? Should I offend your eyes or your nose, please don't be resentful.´

He just didn't get it, did not stop insulting me. If my new friend had not shown up, I would have guaranteed a corpse. As it was, he patted me on the shoulder and took his leave almost politely.

´You shouldn't play with your life, Will! I know this guy, he is out of your league.´

I laughed. ´And he knuckles under to you?´

´That's for reasons I can't tell you. Something to do with my past.´

´A payoff?´

But he did not react to that.

We decided to go see the girl. When we arrived at the funeral parlor, we believed half the city must have congregated there. We had to wait for half an hour until we were admitted. I couldn't restrain myself and broke into tears. Through the haze of tears, I recognized Peter. He stared at me with large eyes. ´I'm happy that you're saying goodbye to her.´

I nodded at him. ´What brings you here? Shouldn't you be with your family these days?´

´That's over´ he said with a sad look. ´The girl has broken my heart.´

Mr. McMahon joined us. He shook my hand and that of my unknown friend. ´Peter is staying with me for a few days.´

´You can tell them the truth by all means´ Peter whispered. ´I don't feel ashamed doting on this girl.´

´A corpse?´ This remark slipped out of my mouth, after all it was in accordance with the facts.

´My wife doesn't want to see me anymore. I am only talking about this girl.´

I handed over the records he had lent me to the doctor. He passed them to the man without a name straight away.

´To what do I owe the honor?´

Peter shrugged his shoulders.

´I wonder about things and would like my thoughts to be spread. I ask myself every minute every goddamn day since the girl died which facts lie behind this death.´

´She isn't dead, is she? I can see her in my dreams, how she is crossing the street...This girl is alive!´

I knew these antics of the stranger already.

´If someone imagines something, he's hard to dissuade. I'm just the same. The three of us are left cornered with our doubts. The case is closed for the police and won't be reopened. There must be specific starting points for a murder investigation and those are not on hand. A terrible accident and that's it.´

Mr. McMahon invited us for dinner. It was not a full-blown cocktail reception, but I had nothing against a little schnapps. The stranger, the doctor and I also stuffed ourselves, too. Such a feast is something great. Afterwards I packed up my belongings and took my leave of my host and his wife.

´Where will you rest your head?´ The mortician made no pretence about his curiosity.

´I find myself something every night. The church is almost always open, no one complains there if I stretch out on one of the pews. Church asylum, so to say.´

Mr. McMahon and the stranger who might as well be a stranger to himself found that side-splitting.

In the evening, I preferably sit in this regular place. I am served a nightcap which is on the house. Today the proprietor stands in front of me and points to my notepad.

´Are you writing a novel, monsieur?´

He knows I have been a teacher in my former life. I tried to convey a yearning for literature to the children.

´Not this time, Bobby! I am drifting with my thoughts; the day is long and the language wants verbalism.´

We then play a little at cards. Bobby is in a very good mood.

Rumor has it that you have developed your own theories regarding this story with the girl. It is supposed to have been a conspiracy. Men in black have finished off the girl.´

I am delighted. ´Amazing what kind of weird theories are being interpreted. One doesn't quite believe what the Other presumes and tells a Third what a Fourth is thinking to himself, until everyone thinks I'm off my rocker. Oh well, the last thing is quite true, but not in the way that is rumored. Truth has hidden in a closet and must be coaxed out of there. But that isn't quite so easy. I'm sticking to it and the citizens of Willoughby will build me a memorial one day.´

## *1933/12/29, Diary of the Mortician*

I should not have let him leave. He returned in the company of two policemen. They asked me whether he was staying with me at present. ´Yes, he is my guest´, I affirmed. ´Well, this man has run riot. He sat at a table with two weird types and made allegations we should follow up. We are considering putting him under arrest. He could pose a danger.´ I laughed quietly. One of my best friends, a criminal? ´Listen, gentlemen, I will vouch for this man. He is in an exceptional situation these days, beyond question. But he could never hurt a fly.´ The taller, younger of the policemen scrutinized me. So far, he had not spoken a single word, but that changed suddenly. ´Tell your friend what you told us, Mister!´ Six eyes rested on the doctor, who had always enjoyed the full trust in Willoughby.

´I feel guilty, there's nothing to be done about that. This girl and I, we were meant for each other. I asked her to be my wife. I wanted to leave my old life behind, everything was ready for the elopement. She had packed her suitcase, I confessed my love to her. We talked a lot. She was so beautiful, so unique. I had never met a girl like her. I was prepared to give up everything for this girl. My surgery, my family, my good reputation. We wanted to go to New York. Then something unexpected happened. I did not kill her, but maybe she couldn't ultimately understand my request, didn't want to let my family slip down into the void. I am responsible for her death, even if I didn't kill her.´ The older policeman nodded at me. ´You heard what he said. That's quite convincing, isn't it? Maybe the mystery is thereby solved. This distinguished doctor was driven by love for the girl so much that he promised her heaven on earth. The stranger couldn't handle that and in a sudden irrational act she threw herself in front of the train.´

For the last time, no! This story could hardly be more incredible!

´You just have to ask his wife. He was planning to attend Christmas Mass. He was with his family the whole time. When would he have had time to spend with this girl? To promise her all kinds of things that he would not be able to keep anyway? Why are you telling such nonsense?´

Peter suddenly broke into tears. He admitted everything. This girl had turned his head. He had no reason for staying alive anymore. The story was made up after all.

After that the matter was resolved in the following hours. Peter's wife confirmed what I had stated. There was no doubt about it that my friend could have nothing to do with the death of the girl. His imagination had run wild with him. He needed my help. I explained to him that he need not worry. He could stay with me as long as he liked. The conversations dragged on till after midnight. At last Peter retired to the guest room and for the first time in days he slept in a bed, did not keep vigil by the body. I had told him of the planned inscription, of the funeral, for which I bear the sole responsibility. He wants to share the costs, which I agreed upon after a short discussion. Afterwards he was a little pacified.

Now I'm sitting here shaking my head. What impact had this girl caused in the few hours that she lingered in Willoughby? Droves of people are taking their leave of her still. I have fixed the date of the funeral for the 6th of January. Until January 5th, the deceased will remain laid out at the funeral parlor. Perhaps someone who can supply personal details will get in touch after all. There's a bottle of wine in front of me. Peter had had one too many, shouted out untruths. He wanted to draw attention to himself; I know his two companions well enough, have even wined and dined them a short while ago. How many people are wondering why it came to this tragedy? And how many people have developed plausible theories? The girl is dead, what use is it to speculate which surrounding circumstances her death has had? A shadow was supposed to have been seen. Has the devil personally lent a hand, because Willoughby is such an ideal place to cause trouble? I have just raised my glass to myself. Is that the aim of this tragedy? To drive people to insanity, to get a peaceful town into the headlines? This poor guy would have gone to prison for a strange girl, would have done penance there. He still imagines continuing to love the girl. A love affair that couldn't be more one-sided. He must see reason again at some point! He cannot chance antagonizing all citizens of Willoughby. He has already ruined his good reputation as a doctor. How does he want to make his living in the future, sustain his family? He cannot stay at my place forever. The girl's funeral will bring him back to his senses, I am convinced of that. He can't stand at her graveside day and night and cry his heart out then. He will tell himself eventually that he has a responsibility towards his family and himself. I am hoping for that.

# SECOND PROTOCOL

A few days have passed, but the mystery surrounding the dead girl of Willoughby remains unsolved. The police have closed the file. It cannot be ascertained without doubt whether it was a case of suicide or a tragic accident. There is a lack of evidence for a murder. Definite is that the girl will be interred. James McMahon's funeral parlor will pay for the cost of the burial service. Through the provision of donations on behalf of the population of our lovely town an inscription of the gravestone can be counted on which will be likewise understood as a commemoration of the deceased. The girl is still the main conversational topic. Wherever several people come together to share news, the fate of the girl will be referred to.

Many people have taken their leave from the girl. Tears have been shed. Supposedly there are men whom the girl has thus impressed that they cannot get over this loss. The day of the funeral is already fixed: January 6th, 1934. There is still hope that someone who knows the girl will come forward. The daily newspapers everywhere are going head over heels with reports about a tragedy, focusing on an unknown young woman. Who is the deceased? Why did she take the bus to Willoughby? Did she deliberately choose suicide? Was she being followed and did she throw herself in front of the train out of desperation? The craziest theories are being fabricated, but none of them seems to hold a trace of credibility. Wild speculations, rumors of egregious magnitude are going around. The death of the girl is being raised to the rank of a sensation. We citizens of Willoughby are shocked by this misfortune, but do not connive with people who want to make money from the event. It is not allowed to take photos of the laid-out deceased. The search does not necessarily need the image of the dead woman. Clues ensue merely through the secured, by now widely known effects that were in the girl's possession. Also by an exact personal description and a very good, almost lifelike drawing.

It's the lull before the storm. It won't be long before a lengthy funeral procession will accompany the girl on her way to her last resting place. The casket is said to be already carpentered. The exact location of the grave has already been fixed. Anyone wanting to pay their respect to the dead girl has time to do so until January $5^{th}$. Maybe till then, the name of the deceased will be known, but in any case, the girl will be buried in the cemetery of Willoughby.

*What lies behind the development of a story? How do the threads run together? And where does inspiration come from in the first place?*

*The narrator permitted himself to reflect on his way of looking at things. He left no room for any doubt about the man whom he hadn't sent packing but sent to Willoughby instead. And for purely egotistical reasons, he has gained my full sympathy.*

## The Narrator, 2013

There, I'm meddling again. I am making an appearance in my own story. Is that wise or will it even be to my disadvantage? Alfred has read through the notes.

'Great, great, my dear fellow!' was his opinion. He could not give me any constructive criticism. That would be asking too much of him. I converse with him; however, the communication runs one-sided. He is the receiver, the frequency from his perspective may be jammed. Still, it would be unreasonable to stop. I have been busying myself with a self-chosen project for a few months. I am doing this to myself at an age where others just think of dying. I will lie in a coffin long enough later and recuperate from the struggles of a life which I could never quite comprehend. Right now, I am still capable of dedicating myself to a story.

Why did I make just this tragedy the subject of my contemplation? A remote acquaintance told me of it. He is a writer too, does a lot of research and is on the lookout for unusual stories. He encountered this *"Girl in Blue"* on the Internet. At my request he printed out a few articles for me and a photo of the grave on the cemetery of Willoughby as well as a picture of the girl herself. I was delighted, enraptured, a transcendental sensation. I had not gotten over the death of my wife yet, but I was celebrating my resurrection. From one moment to the next, I was again the man my wife had not been able to break free from all her life. I used to tell her the most outrageous stories day after day and she listened to them with pleasure. She loved my stories, she loved me.

The question is whether I am not misled. Sending this Edi to Willoughby! A rather inexperienced middle-aged man who is prepared to leave his old life behind. Edi could be a copy of myself. He behaves like a bull in a china shop, at least that's my impression. I have never been to Willoughby and it can be ruled out that I will ever make it there. Therefore, I imagine what the people there might be like. I invent destinies which more or less intertwine. Starting point is and always remains the *"Girl in Blue"*. Doesn't every woman deserve a memorial? If I do my utmost to compose an obituary for this poor unfortunate, which far exceeds the traditional dimension, then I am probably doing this in lieu of all the unhappy women who left this planet before their time. This girl provides fodder for conversation up to this day, not only in Willoughby. The story has transgressed the borders of the United States. Japanese, Koreans, probably Austrians too take a long journey upon themselves. They stand in front of the grave of the *"Girl in Blue"* and pray for the salvation of her soul. The grave is always adorned with flowers. This girl, whose identity was only established decades after her death, connects people from all over the world.

I cannot avoid admitting a certain obsessiveness to myself. The dead girl has taken possession of me. She is reaching out for me, sometimes scaring me. I will possibly meet her in the afterlife. Only then will I know how this horrible tragedy came about that ended her young life. I am partially projecting this obsession into the characters whom I am encountering like a contemporary witness. There are so many secrets that do not find their way from the darkness into light. I will do my bit to pay tribute to a creature that seems to have enchanted a whole town.

Alfred was here again. He smiled the whole time, even when he spilled coffee on his trousers. I showed him her photo.

´Pretty, very beautiful ´, he said, open-mouthed. Does the beauty of the soul also show itself in the mortal remains? Is the immortal soul not only reflected in the eyes, but in the whole body? If I look at her photo, I see her as a walker. She saunters through Vienna, smiling at everyone she encounters. No one yells at her to refrain from doing so. No one thinks her gaiety is impertinent. The city of Vienna is being transformed by her existence. It must have been exactly like that in Willoughby! I confided to Alfred what was going through my head. Then a miracle happened!

´This must have been a girl that just existed on earth to hold up a mirror to people's faces. Some people began to hate their reflection and just an instant later they awakened to new life.´

Yes, that is what Alfred said. He contemplated her photo for minutes, then he looked at his watch.

'It is time. Time to go.'

Then he left me. He left me and he left this world. His death came so suddenly that at first, I couldn't comprehend it fully.

Now I am waiting for the doctor. He will arrange for everything else. What an ending, what a death! I am staying in another room; the deceased has his eyes open and I cannot muster the strength to close his eyes. Alfred was a little younger than me. He was suffering from dementia but he died in full command of his mental faculties. I will not cease writing this story. I don't just owe this to the girl, but also to Alfred, who encouraged me to start with the transcription of the story in the first place. And my wife will always be in my heart, her quintessential ghost is sitting on my shoulder and is watching me write. One day I will have finished, that's the hope I have. Then my obsession will have dissipated. I will be released, will surrender myself fully to life. My wife, Alfred and the "*Girl in Blue*" form the invincible trio that bestows the vital energy upon me that will carry me the rest of my life. And in the afterlife, we will be a quartet that will be acquainted in all eternity.

*The narrator's fondness for the young woman, whom he granted a strong personality for all her fragility, is a common thread throughout our novel. She might have been a feminist of exceptional characteristic in the year 1946, of which we will presently learn.*

## The Girl as a Young Woman, 1946

The separation from Richard opened a new life for me. Carl temporarily moved in with me. Brother and sister under one roof. He didn't interfere. I could do as I pleased. If Richard shows up, he's in for it. Carl outmuscles him by far. I am finally able to think entirely free again. Richard has inhibited me far too long. He managed to estrange me from myself. I was just his doll, his puppet. Every decision had to be accounted for. I had no best friend, his jealousy prevented any more intimate contact with other people. Whenever he wanted, I instantly had to be ready to serve him in whatever form he desired. This supposedly is not uncommon amongst couples. Still, in retrospect I am aghast at how much he manipulated me. Personal contact with my parents and Carl was kept within severe limits. Richard governed my life.

Nowadays I am feeling as good as I haven't felt in a very long time. Carl and I often play cards or converse about literary works in the evening. It can't be avoided that every now and then we talk about the *"Girl in Blue"*. I am convinced that I have arrived at a point prior to the one with the encounter on that 24th December 1933. Those few seconds of emotional attachment to the girl catapulted me into an abyss that I am slowly digging myself out of. I cannot yet claim to be healed. I am in therapy in Peter's practice. He is a very good therapist and knows all too well about my psychological condition. He has suffered badly from the events himself. I am traveling back in time. The girl's funeral was imminent. I was blaming myself for the death of this enchanting beauty. A demon had taken possession of me and ordered me to annihilate the girl. This conviction weakened my childlike soul with concentrated force. I deliberated whether I even wanted to attend the funeral. After all I had not had the heart to see the girl on her death bed. The fear of being changed into a demon damned for all eternity had prevented the farewell. But maybe everything was a delusion? I was a fun-loving child, but different from the other children. If a demon is searching a soul in Willoughby, it would be mine!

I spent a sleepless night. The girl appeared before my bed and whispered to me:

'It's all right! You need not worry. I haven't bewitched you. You are predestined to make something special of your life! Be so kind and devote yourself to the aesthetic things. I know what great talents are slumbering within you. You can draw, write and sing beautifully. The world lies at your feet. I will not keep you from becoming yourself. Trust yourself and have trust in me!'

I could have jumped with joy and begun a new life back then. But I believed it was a deceptive maneuver. Indeed, I was cheerful for a few seconds, but with the disappearance of the apparition I reverted to my old fears. I lay in bed with a vacant stare like a corpse and asked myself why I was alive.

My parents and Carl wanted to attend the funeral. On that morning we prayed a lot. My dad put a wonderful dress on my bed. Internally I was as agitated as never before in my life. No one bears me ill will. No, I just convinced myself of that, because it took the pressure off my chest. An hour before the funeral my mother stroked my thick hair.

'Everything is all right, love! You'll see, you'll be relieved!'

I felt the tears rise and ran to my room. I also compare notes about this day with Carl. He tells me his view of the events.

'I was scared stiff of the funeral procession. And when I imagined the coffin being lowered into the earth, too dreadful to imagine! Believe me, I wasn't being a hero, on the contrary! But it was my duty to go along on this last journey of the unknown girl. I had seen her lie there so peacefully. She let my heart grow calm.'

And then they went. Carl, mother and father. All of Willoughby paid their respects to the girl, only I still hesitated. What had I done that I was so reluctant to join the people whom the girl had wished a Merry Christmas and all the best? I would have liked to vanish into thin air, to be re-born into a different universe and to have known nothing about the life I had led before.

Now, these doubts have disappeared. I wonder at having been such a silly girl. Was there any other person in Willoughby that had harbored similar thoughts to mine? No, I couldn't imagine that. I was cursed, a demon caused my inner distraction. By now I have come closer to that person whom the apparition prophesized me that night. I am mad about writing, devote myself to literature, even keep my own bookshop as heiress to my father. I also have a knack for drawing. I illustrate some of my poems. Richard used to laugh about it, but fortunately that's over for good. Yes, without doubt I can sing too. My mother even thinks I have what it takes to make a career as a singer. The few appearances at small events ensured thunderous applause. Yes, I ultimately want to become the person I am destined to be by God. That I want to promise God and myself.

*The stranger was on the brink of decamping. He confided profound thoughts about death to his diary. The funeral of the "Girl in Blue" was about to put an end to his circuit in Willoughby.*

## The Stranger, 1934

Who is actually being consigned to the grave? A poor soul? That is the wrong answer. Because the soul of the girl lives on, is part of the big picture somewhere in the heavens. This doctor has convinced me that I don't have to feel haunted any more. If the deceased appears, then it can only be a case of wishful thinking on my part. Therefore, I have no reason to stay here.

The girl and I arrived in Willoughby at the same time. We are both keeper of a secret. No one will be able to elicit from me why I frighten people who are used to a sedate life like a ghost. I love to cause a stir. My indifference, my taciturnity and my cluelessness make me a misfit. This is the role of my life. Wherever I stop, I act similarly. Call it a psychological study, if you set eyes on these notes. I am not enough for myself, I must define myself by playing a part.

During the last days I have grown pensive. The people of Willoughby have opened my barriers with their cordiality. I am ready to give up my play-acting, but I can't do it. The show must go on, it mustn't die. Mrs. Judd is harboring me. In the evening we sit at the kitchen table and allow ourselves to listen to each other. We tell stories. Miss Judd is shocked about the death of the girl. Her warmth, her kindness, her joviality, her love of life.

´She did not kill herself. Something went wrong, one cogwheel engaged incorrectly with the next. Then the whole machine fell apart.´ I don't hear for the first time that doubts about the suicide of the young woman persist. But even my friend, the buddy without a jacket and shirt, is tired of accusing God and the world because a murder isn't being treated as such. Bad enough that a person met her death who buzzed around people like a dayfly. Like the fly, the girl did not know what was in store for her.

After the funeral I'll take to my heels. People elsewhere are waiting to enjoy my play-acting. Willoughby isn't the hub of the world, even if the press is hyping the case as a sensation. I see the girl before me, as she stopped off at Ms. Judd with a buoyant spirit. A little later she appeared in a blue dress, blue shoes and white blouse in church. She prayed for a long time. I was one of the people who enjoyed being wished a Merry Christmas. That is the whole story. Everything else is wild speculation, a fancy to attribute another face to death. Who am I to act up as the girl's judge? She went her own way, which no one else knew. Maybe her death is a staging. And we, the survivors, erect a memorial to this shady creature.

I am growing sick with yearning. Death is reaching out his claws for me, too. To escape him, I must move on. Death finds his victims everywhere. And how many people died on battlefields, were murdered, massacred, messed up, disposed of, liquidated? The girl's death is tragic, but she did not suffer, at least that's what I believe. Death must have been instantaneous. The girl did not scream in pain. The crossing over into the other life was fast and painless. Is it beyond belief that the girl had a happy death?

Before I use my malicious tongue, I'll be long gone. I don't need to bid anyone goodbye. I came out of nowhere and that's where I'm going back to. I won't leave a void. Willoughby doesn't need a person like me for good. Mrs. Judd views that differently. I could be a model citizen of this town, she thinks. While all other men just show off and hide their hearts on their tongues, I have the makings to be mayor. I appreciate this adulation, but the dear Mrs. Judd is mistaken. No one deserves it more than me to be chased out of town. I have deceived them all, all except Mrs. Judd. The funeral will be my last adventure on this trip. I will say farewell to the one person who is my only connection to Willoughby. In the short time of my detour to Willoughby the town and its inhabitants have remained alien to me. I didn't find access. I don't except Mrs. Judd. Even though I was prepared not to act a masquerade for her, I still did not get closer to her by an inch.

Tomorrow the time has come. I will be present and won't raise the veil. That's the similarity with the dead girl. I will once more see the people with whom I could spend some time together. People that I unnerved by my belief that the girl was still alive. They will probably be glad to be rid of me. After all I'm just a stranger with a penchant for drama, not a chronicler of events. I don't want to be a spoilsport, Willoughby doesn't deserve that. The truth will come to light someday. The doctor's records are too confused. He's a wacko like me. We are brothers in spirit. I wish for him and the citizens of Willoughby that they use the events as an opportunity to face one another with respect and courtesy. The girl shall serve as their role model. Maybe she has just come to Willoughby to herald the start of a new, better time.

*80 years had passed after the death of the girl. The Austrian from the capital city made an extraordinary experience which will leave a mark on him for life. The records that had been placed at his disposal paled in the face of the reality which he saw himself confronted with. Willoughby had become a second home to him.*

## A European in Willoughby, 2013

I had no difficulty at all preferring Willoughby to my family. My wife called me again yesterday. She screamed at me so that I was almost tempted to split up with her right there on the telephone. But for the time being I was considerate of my children, I tried to calm down the woman for whom I once left another.

´Not a chance´, she just said. ´Not a chance! If you don't light the candles on the Christmas tree tomorrow, you can look for another place to stay.´ Today I'm not sitting together with my family in Vienna and enjoying a few pleasant hours. The day after Christmas Eve we always used to be in high spirits, took a walk, went to the movies, even made an appearance at my in-laws. Yesterday I cheated Vienna of myself. Willoughby has me under its spell. My research has not moved forward an inch. I am studying the records that have been newly handed to me, but that is of no help. Something abnormal singles out this town, where this horrible disaster happened 80 years and a day ago. None of the inhabitants wanted to get too close to the story. What was once the talk of the town has grown to be a myth. Josephine, the *"Girl in Blue"*, is part of Willoughby. She is presumed to be on this or that street corner. Many a person sees her standing in front of her grave whispering words that cannot be understood. She is wearing those clothes she was buried in. Karen is the only person who exchanges more than a few words with me. She has devoted herself to the girl for decades. She hasn't left Willoughby even for a day. She did not want to disappoint the girl, has adorned her grave with flowers every week. She dedicated her whole life to the memory of the girl. She herself got the short end of the stick, but she perceives this completely differently.

´Every person has their very own purpose to fulfil´, she told me yesterday, a few hours prior to Christmas Mass. ´And my purpose is to preserve this girl in my heart and to do everything so her memory won't fall into oblivion. I am something like Josephine's advocate. What do you think how many people have asked me about her? I am not as pigheaded as you might think. Yes, sometimes I shoo away people from her grave, because I see Josephine's tranquility threatened. You know, my life hasn't been a calm lake that I've swum in without haste. There have been many waves, people have laughed at me, have doubted my state of mind. But I have got things straightened out with myself, I dare to offer you my arm so you will escort me to Christmas Mass.´

Karen's acquaintance is my greatest pleasure these days. I like listening to her. She opens her heart to me in lucid moments and I can see the girl who had an extraordinary experience with an unknown young woman all these years ago. These few minutes have steered her life into a direction from which she has never deviated again. She did not want to take another road anymore. And she doesn't believe that she has missed out on anything in her life.

The church was filled to capacity. I held Karen's hand during almost the whole of Christmas Mass. She sang her heart out, I on the other hand was something of a silent witness. The clergyman mentioned the *"Girl in Blue"* in his sermon. He told her story, reminded the community to pray for Josephine. And then it happened: I saw her sitting three rows in front of me pushed right to the edge of the pew. She turned back and looked at me with hazel eyes. I wanted to say something but she put her index finger on her lips. Karen pressed my hand. After the end of Christmas Mass there was a small communal drink.

´She made contact with you, didn't she?´

I kissed Karen on both cheeks.

´Yes, she smiled at me. I could sense the warm-heartedness she exuded. It was a wonderful feeling.´

Back at home I instantly sat down at my desk and wrote down my thoughts. What I had so far only read in records has now penetrated my own life. The young woman radiates her love to the people that remember her beyond death. I can only interpret the silence of the women and men of Willoughby thus that they want to keep their relations with the girl to themselves. I can't blame them for it. And I will do likewise, and tell no one of this incredible encounter. This secret must be guarded like a treasure. I will soon put these records that I am writing down now into a safe. My chronicler will have the task of having the safe opened 20 years after my death at the earliest, so that the truth comes to light. Because I don't want to take this unique occurrence that has happened to me to my grave forever and always. The following generations will be aware of the fact that there is more than man's destructive power. A young woman has had a significant effect upon the course of history. She has charged Karen with guarding her legacy. And Karen in turn has handed me the key that will save humanity from its decline in the distant future. I don't feel like continuing my boring family life in Vienna anymore. What was originally planned as a small trip has become an adventure that will continue until my life's end. I am sorry for my wife and children, who don't have a husband and father anymore. But one day they will understand which circumstances have led to this radical decision.

## *1934/01/07, Diary of the Mortician*

No one had waited for this day. But the whole of Willoughby was up and about. Even early in the morning, a special atmosphere was noticeable. It was very mild for a winter's day. No one would have to freeze. I had breakfast with Peter. He could only wrest himself free from the unknown girl with difficulty.

´You'll see that everything will be all right. The last days were hard on you and your family. But reason will triumph. Your feelings for the stranger will cool down.´

Peter looked at me with vacant eyes. He was completely tired out. ´I owe it to myself not to forget this young woman. I recorded her death, determined the cause of death. I was up half the night on that Christmas Eve, admiring the beauty of the girl. Today she will be consigned to the grave and I can only beg you to grant her a wonderful burial.´

Peter couldn't eat a thing, just drank a little coffee. ´It'll soon be over. I want to thank you again for bearing part of the expenses.´

He stared in the direction of the window. Voices filtered into the parlor. Journalists were waiting for me to open the funeral home.

´I can only thank you for giving me shelter. My wife and my children are threatening to refuse me admittance into my own home forever.´

By and large 3000 people took their leave of the girl. They would have flocked in even right before the funeral if I had permitted that. I opened the door and a cluster of people talked insistently to me. I couldn't understand a word.

'Please be so kind and keep calm. I am not available for interviews. You must be patient. I have lots of preparations still. And I ask you to refrain from taking photographs during the obsequies.'

Then I set out for the cemetery.

The room was brightly lit. People sat down on rows of benches. People who already had had to process numerous deaths in their family circle. In a minimum of time, the girl had become part of the greater family of the citizens of Willoughby. Nothing linked these people to the girl except a few shared moments. These moments however had touched them so deeply that they were now crying. Peter sat in the front row and kept on sobbing. Old and young, poor and rich, healthy and sick people commemorated a young woman whose life had come to an end in the midst of Willoughby. The clergyman did not talk much, for a few seconds it was literally dead silent. Then, out of the blue, that man who had crept around Willoughby like a shadow for a few days, maybe even since Christmas Eve, rose to speak.

'She's alive, listen, you citizens of Willoughby, she's alive!' With that, he caused turmoil. A few seasoned men wanted to pounce on him but were held back by their wives. Soon the noise level decreased. I prepared myself to discharge my duties.

The coffin, which my best man has carpentered, has turned out splendidly. The girl must feel comfortable in it. She can stretch out her arms and have a good yawn if she feels like it. I have to smile inwardly at this thought. Hundreds of people accompany the *"Girl in Blue"* on her last journey. I am watching closely if an awkward situation might develop. Especially at funerals, unforeseen incidents may happen that one must react to intuitively. Fortunately, it is different this time. Everything takes place in a rather civilized manner. Peter is holding a bouquet of flowers in his hand. He is proceeding with a bowed head. His wife is walking a few feet behind him, flanked by their two children. When the procession stops, Peter's wife steps close to him. She whispers something in his ear. He gives her a kiss on the cheek. My employees are doing their best. Finally, the coffin is being lowered into the darkness on pulleys. Now the moment has come where a last glance can be cast at the coffin. One, two hours later the coffin will be covered with earth. I am proud that everything is going smoothly. No one collapses in front of the grave, no one screams or runs riot.

I don't know how long the funeral has taken. It seemed like an eternity to me. The *"Girl in Blue"* has found her last resting place on the cemetery of Willoughby. The journalists have remained quiet, they haven't tried to take a single photo. The morning gazette reports exclusively about the funeral. Surprisingly, piety is preserved. It must be hoped that the events won't be exaggerated elsewhere. After all, by now half the world knows what inexplicable casualty has happened in Willoughby on Christmas Eve of the year 1933. I must be prepared to be cross-examined sooner or later. Because I have done my work well, I will be able to answer the journalists' questions composedly. A publisher has inquired whether I wouldn't like to write a book about the *Mystery of Willoughby*. Far be it from me to concern myself exceedingly with this sad story. As a mortician, I'm not down on my uppers, after all I'll never run out of customers.

The inscription on the gravestone will be engraved in a few days. The wording is already fixed:

In Memory of The Girl in Blue

Killed by Train

December 24, 1933

# MAGIC

*The third part of our novel mostly takes place in the year 1963. The records that have been leaked to me are written from the perspective of a woman who is well-known to us. But my old acquaintance, the narrator of this story, surprised me enormously by who else appears on the scene. 30 years after the dreadful accident, a new chapter was opened that we can take an interest in. The "Girl in Blue" had lost nothing of her allure.*

## Karen, 1963

It has been nearly two years since I received a letter. This happens very rarely. Because the letter was addressed to me personally and it was neither a request for payment nor a bill. When I saw the signature, I was completely taken by surprise.

*Dear Karen, I don't know if you remember me. Long before the war I was a guest in your town. I prowled the streets, attracted attention by strange behavior. Now I want to reveal myself to you: I was only play-acting. I ended this farce a few hours after the unknown girl's funeral. I have never forgotten this girl. You were still young back then, 12 years old at the most. Research has entailed that I have come across your address. The reason why I am writing to you is a request. I want to come to Willoughby once more. Yes, it has been a long time and the dead should be left in peace. But the shadows won't let me go. I ask you to relay a message to Will, Peter and Mr. McMahon that I would be grateful to them if we could meet one day at the grave of the girl in the cemetery and bring the whole matter to a close. I am sure you know what I mean. Greetings from Walter Longstone.*

An internationally renowned actor turns out to be the person who caused turmoil in Willoughby for a while back then. I had to re-read the letter a few times. After I had digested the words, I confronted Peter and James with Walter's wish. They immediately agreed to follow the call. It was more difficult to find out Will's whereabouts. He had left Willoughby a few months after the accident. But it proved to be a stroke of luck that Peter owns the only published book of the unappreciated author. It took a few weeks but his telegraph was answered. Now it was necessary to start the preparations. An enormous tension took hold of me. To talk about the events after so many years seemed like a twist of fate to me. I visit the grave of the girl nearly every day, that hasn't changed to this day. One day I developed a high fever, fell seriously sick. I had to postpone the meeting with Walter. He phoned me every few days and asked about my circumstances. With a few months delay he then showed up in Willoughby. I was a bit unsteady on my feet, so Walter had to support me with his arm on the way to the cemetery. He prayed there silently to himself until he unburdened himself to me.

'I am glad to be here. I struggled with myself for a few years. I thought the matter was over and done with. But the girl has haunted me right my dreams. And your family was friends with Peter's family back then after all…that's how it happened. I'm still the clueless slob I was. Yes, I made a career as an actor, featured in a few successful films. But that is nothing compared to the emptiness I feel inside which I could never fill. I want to tell you, Peter, Will and James a story. Oh, and how excited I am to see all of you again!'

In the evening we shared a meal at Peter's. We raised our glasses and thought of the unknown girl. Finally, the conversation got a little stagnant. James had brought a photo album that he had not dared to show anyone before. In a few pictures the dead girl is seen lying in her coffin. She wore those beautiful clothes. The *"Girl in Blue"*. I had been too cowardly to take my leave of her back then. At the sight of the photographs, I burst into tears, couldn't control myself at all. We finally agreed on visiting the cemetery the coming afternoon. Will had announced himself. Walter took quarters in a nice pension. He kindly refused Peter's offer to stay with his family. I turned night into day. I knew I would not be able to sleep so I sat down at my desk and wrote down whatever went through my head. It was nearly 30 years ago that this calamity shook up Willoughby. Every citizen of our little town knows the story. Not a day passes that some fresh flowers adorn the girl's grave. I am part of the whole. If there is something that singles me out, then it is the relationship to this woman. I have truly failed at many things in my life. My relationships with men always came to a soon end. I allowed no one to come near me, behaving like a spinster. I perceived this event and its consequences for me like a curse. I couldn't help myself but complain to my Maker. How could he have let it happen that my life would be so unilateral? Walter must have been better off, even if he didn't want to admit it. We all had a heavy load to carry. I nearly couldn't carry mine anymore at all. Sometimes it weighed so heavy upon my shoulders that it took my breath away. Maybe Walter's letter arrived just on time. I was on the brink of going completely crazy. I must have fallen asleep sometime at my desk after all. I woke up the next morning with a throbbing head. Pills against the headache were the only chance to survive the day. In a few hours, the wheel of time will be turned back. The day will be December 24th, 1933. I couldn't eat a thing. I lay in bed curled up like an embryo until noon. I felt chilly. Just don't be sick again, I told myself. Today is too important to be spent just in bed. Therefore, I forced myself to get up. I drank a lot of tea, listened to the radio, read the paper. Then I looked at my watch. It was time to depart. I wrapped myself up well on this mild spring day. It was necessary not to run out of steam.

*The stranger has been given a face 30 years after the accident. He unmasked himself and behind this mask the person Walter came to light. A person whose peculiar performance in Willoughby has felt suspicious to himself, too. The charade had found an end with considerable delay.*

## Walter, the Actor, recounts (1963)

I was the first on site. Not a trace of the others. My headache was bearable, but I felt unabatedly weak and a hot tropical storm seemed to unfurl in my insides. But I resisted my urge to leave this place and retire to bed. Peter finally considerately stepped closer to me and made a worried face when he looked at me. 'You should take better care of yourself. Don't you dare be irresponsible towards yourself. Life is too precious.' We stood in front of the grave in silence until James arrived. He joined us without speaking a word. Just a little later, the initiator of our gathering appeared. Walter, contrary to the long-time residents, was dressed very fashionably. I wasn't feeling well at all. Several times I thought I would collapse at the next moment. Will patted me on the shoulder. He must have sneaked up from behind.

´That's not funny at all!´ I said.

´You face is white as a sheet´ said Will and stroked both my cheeks. ´We should get this over with quickly.´

´I am very obliged to you that you have come here. You can take my word for it that I have dreaded this day for years. To once more dwell in this place. Willoughby! I was a seeker when I combed through the town on this Christmas Day in 1933. My first memory is Mrs. Judd's pension. The young woman vanished into the house. There and then the idea manifested itself to pay her my respects. I waited until she ventured out again. The girl had changed. She was beaming and not at all surprised that I addressed her. Hours later I imagined seeing her again. I followed her trail until I heard the rattle of a train. We don't know what exactly happened. This accident is a mystery until today. The young woman lay there, dead. And I decided to pretend as if I had the purpose not to be willing to accept her death. I acted like a madman, like someone who's taken leave of his senses. Well, you know this part of the story to a large extent. I am sorry that I double-crossed you and generally all citizens of Willoughby. This mummery arose from my wish to develop further as an actor. I dreamed about belonging to those successful players whose names are known to half the world. Yes, it was a form of megalomania!´

´I left like a ghost which is still chained to the town. I never shed those chains. The swiftly ensuing successes as an actor changed nothing about the fact that I had nightmares. I looked out of the train window and the girl's face changed into a skull. I woke up countless times bathed in sweat. I want to finally purge myself of this story that has never relinquished its hold on me. I want to be ready to bid adieu to the girl, to no longer torment her with my thoughts. And I have brought something along which I recommend to you.´

´We were linked to each other by an invisible tie back then and nothing has changed about that until today. The manuscript I am handing over for you to read contains my whole life. It is not an autobiography but a life of suffering. I have raised the girl from the dead, written her story. You will see that you are part of the drama yourselves. After a lengthy preface, you emerge as characters of a play. The roles intended for each of you all have a connection to the tragically killed woman. I have exclusively selected scenes which I have experienced with you in the few days during which I paid a visit to Willoughby. I'd be much obliged if you would take this story, this unconventional play, to heart. Maybe it will be of use as an elucidation, as a liberation from a straightjacket. I have returned here because I have the feeling that it is time to be able to breathe freely again. This state of being constantly involved in one cause which haunts me, is making my life miserable.´

During Walter's monologue, none of the listeners had interposed even a single word. We all were probably both surprised and shocked. During those minutes, I even forgot the heat rising from my innards. Peter put an end to it.

´I see that Karen is unwell. Thank you, my dear fellow, for dishing out this story. I will read it in any case, I promise you that! And when we've all read it, we will meet here again. It's important that Karen gets well again. She probably overtaxed herself.´

With that said, he supported me on the way to my small house. Several times I thought I would not make it, but after what felt like an eternity I was lying in bed.

'You're running a high fever!' Peter cautioned me. 'You should sleep a lot now and I'll fetch you some meds right away which will do you good!' I must have fallen asleep right away.

I dreamt of a film in which I played the lead. I was the *"Girl in Blue"*. But I wasn't dead, but instead made all of Willoughby laugh.

My cheerfulness ended abruptly when I faced myself and said with utter conviction: 'I want to be you again, to be you again, d'you hear?'

Peter was sitting next to my bed when I woke up. 'You've slept for nearly 24 hours, that's very good. Now you must take it easy and stay in bed until you're out of the woods. You know how fast it can happen that death comes knocking.'

I decided to read Walter's manuscript during the few hours of wakefulness. It was outrageous. I could not read more than two or three pages at a time, however. If Walter wanted to hear my impressions of the story, he would have to be patient and put up with a longer stay in Willoughby.

*Now I have reached a point where I suffer with the narrator. The death of his friend had caused a great life crisis. Only the story of the "Girl in Blue" and his effort to achieve a last great success with it kept him alive. He was a writer with heart and soul and never complained about being overtaxed. For this I pay him my greatest respects.*

## The Narrator, 2013

Alfred's funeral made me feel very low. Especially during the last days of his life, we spent almost every day together. Even if he didn't talk very much, he encouraged me. I am not sure if I can manage to finish the last project of my life without him. I have produced a few words. Except for me, the chaplain, the pallbearers and the gravedigger, no one else was present. The farewell took place in complete silence. I miss Alfred. And I know that he is watching me while I am trying to gain a quantum of inspiration. How much time do I have left? Alfred was younger, more vital. He wasn't quite himself, forgot words, couldn't name things anymore.

And what about my energy reserves? I am moving towards an uncertain end. Every story carries infinity within itself. No event remains singular. Everything is connected into a Whole. Incidents are never isolated, always create a link. Thus, my *"Girl in Blue"* will wait for the train in all eternity and will prematurely outwit life. I cling to life. I cling to life so much that I am left in disbelief at having to die soon. My wife is waiting for me, she surely is longing for me. And I am taking my time, won't let go, am not letting myself go. I am digging for a treasure within me that might not even exist.

Kafka and Musil saw themselves as failures. They created world literature without noticing. Kafka felt that he sufficed neither in life nor in writing. Musil wrote like a man possessed, who yet knows that in the end he will face God like a fool. What about me? The numerous stories of my life are behind me. I can't bring myself to write them down any more. I've tried a few times. A story opened up to me, wanted to be told. I have never reached the realization to paint characters so vividly that they would engage in dialogue with me. They stayed unaffected, didn't cry, didn't laugh. Like me, they were detached. I destroyed them with my dispassion. They were no puppets and yet pulled as if by invisible strings. I wrote of spiritual kinship, of inner disturbance, of failure. Every story miscarried. In honor of Kafka and Musil I'll write it down again: I have failed. And yet I am still doing right now what I have always done. I'll have another go. Another time, a last time. *The last bird catches the worm.* That's how some proverb goes, or not? The worm has always been an incentive to me. Now it's wiggling in my beak. I want to scarf it down, to devour it, to make it a part of me.

I have stuck my neck out too far. Alfred could have reined me in, but he let me go ahead.

´Listen, Alfred, what do you think about the whole thing?´ How often did I pose this absurd question? Does my fear dictate my life? I distract myself, tell stories, so I don't have to face the truth. The bitter truth, the final truth, death. Alfred has appeared to me in my dreams almost every night since his death. He talks like he did before his sickness.

´Just stay true to yourself and don't disappoint me!´

Yes, against all circumstances I am still close to myself. They have not managed to chain me. But because of this my fear of death is even stronger. What will await me then? Will I be able to finish my story, to finally come to an end, to finally exclaim: ´Now success is here, now there is no doubt anymore!´ I wish to be myself in the last reality. My wife, Alfred and I will tell each other stories for all eternity. And they won't be stories that will be shrouded in the veil of finitude. In eternity, there is no relativity. Every story is perfect in itself and is waiting to be continued. In this way, every moment, an enormous number of stories come into existence. Oh, exactly that is what I dream of in this life! I am a storyteller and fly into a passion about never coming close to the inner truth. There is no failure in eternity. Kafka, Musil and myself will be relieved of the desire to produce something from the abyss that had been worthlessly deposited there.

There isn't much time left. I will continue the story, even if it cannot succeed. Alfred, like the *"Girl in Blue"*, is over it. I am ready to follow them. But first I still have something left to do. I am dead serious. Towards the end of my earthly existence I have forgotten how to laugh. I have grown as wooden as my characters. They set out into the world and now we sit together at table. Day by day we get up together, breakfast together, go shopping, eat lunch and dinner, watch TV, write, read the paper and retire to bed. We only have each other anymore. Alfred was the last loyal supporter who kept me and my characters company. His death has severed my tie to the world. I float above ground; my characters hover a few feet away from me. I reach out my arms towards them and cannot get hold of them. They are beyond reach. They have the privilege of being independent. Despite the invisible threads I no longer have a hold on them. I want them to live, to finally be alive! No longer a figment of the imagination! I don't want to be back on safe ground, I am too old for that. Will my characters help me, when I can't help myself anymore? Will they let me fall and will they have cast a net so I will have a soft landing?

*Peter, the doctor, and thus the grandfather of Alfred Keanes, whom we know from the described encounters with the young man from Austria, had no reason anymore to relativize his exorbitant egotism of past times. He was finally relieved of his imposed role.*

## The Doctor tells his story (1963)

I was laid low for nearly three weeks and Peter visited me every day to bring me up to date. Will was quartered at his place for the duration of his stay in Willoughby. Walter on the other hand resided at the best hotel. Both were happy to prowl through the streets of this formerly so familiar town once again. I excused myself several times. One day I finally felt able to set foot out of the house for a few steps. And a week later we all found ourselves standing in the cemetery at the unknown girl's grave. Peter had brought along a wicker chair for safety's sake, in case I should have a feeling of faintness.

´Well, I admire your composure, Walter! As a very busy actor you must be sitting on hot coals.´

Walter waved him aside. ´Nah, Peter. I knew what I was getting myself into. Why should my rules always apply to everything?´

That was the cue for Peter to start with his monologue.

´I approve that we are meeting exclusively at the grave. As I know, Walter and Will have a lot to tell each other. But this is a different matter. None of us has dared to even allusively describe our experiences with the event. It was always just about the calamity, the accident, the mystery, our own sensitivities. Walter's play shows how much we have strayed. He cuts to the chase: we stewed in our own juice, wallowed in self-pity, let us get carried away into not wasting a single thought to the girl herself. Who she might have been, what she wanted in Willoughby, why she was prepared to die here? Our shadows hovered over the girl. I was fascinated by this young woman from the very beginning. Yes, I loved her and maybe I still love her even today. But is that of any relevance? I ran against walls day after day, my family didn't recognize me anymore, still worse, I had grown a stranger to myself. My misfortune was the girl's misfortune. I clung to her until she was buried.´

Peter cleared his throat quickly before he continued. I felt a little faint, so I sat down in the provided wicker chair.

´I was thinking of nothing but myself. How terrible it is to be connected forever to that girl. Then I couldn't take it anymore. Eventually it all became too much. Karen knows what I'm talking about. She was my first patient. I've been a therapist for many years. If the accident hadn't happened, then I wouldn't stand before you as a therapist. I had failed as a doctor, as a therapist I wanted to make up for it all. Therefore, I opened a new practice a few years after my misconduct and within a few weeks several new patients gathered. I had soon realized during the training that I primarily needed therapy myself. The analysis of my soul brought to light how much I was suffering. I told my therapist countless times about the burden that drove me crazy. Who was I in this sad play? Walter depicts me as an uncouth person ignorant of himself. I was in the process of digging my own grave.´

Walter stepped up to Peter, hugged him shortly.

´I was hoping for that, that you'd come clean. How far were you prepared to go?´

Peter nodded and kneeled in front of the grave.

´I am deeply indebted to this girl. She showed me that I am just a miserable worm. I did not want to concede to myself to project each_insignificant little matter on the unfortunate woman. If something didn't work out, I instantly blamed it on her. My failed life had just one basis and that was the one-sided love towards a deceased. Can anything be added to this? I think not! You see before you a person who can finally smile at his own visage, that's all.´

I had listened attentively the whole time. Peter and I were friends. James pursued his job as a mortician, nothing would change about that during his lifetime. It surprised me that he of all people began to speak.

´You went out on a limb there with your life confession, Peter! We all appreciate you as a renowned therapist and former doctor. Walter's decision to once more deal with the story helps us get rid of the baggage. I too have something to tell. Given the late hour I'm volunteering to chance the hazard of self-revelation tomorrow, at the same time, in the same place.´

None of the attendants had any objections to that.

When would I be ready to release my soul from its prison? Like all concerned parties I had read Walter's play. My past youth connected me in a special way to the girl. I brooded if I was even able to offer anything beyond truisms? I rested at home. The bookshop could be run without me. My aged father helped me out. I asked myself whether I had always searched for answers only in books? Had I kept the key to my innermost always hidden in a dark corner? What did the many books tell me? I was alone, lonely, sad, forlorn. Was that the punishment for once having fancied to be possessed by a demon? I was very curious to hear the others' reports. If a certain line would be crossed, I wanted to be ready to keep in step. I don't want to be a coward any more. This reticence only makes sick in the long run. Thanks to Walter we have lost our rigidity. By now, I wasn't in treatment with Peter anymore. He made every effort to help me. I was his very first patient and he thought he was indebted to me. He never even divulged the tiniest detail about me. We will stay faithful to each other in our silence.

*The most important witnesses of the events of Dec. 24th, 1933 listened in suspense to the account of James, the mortician. He had something outrageous to tell. Something that weighed on his heart even thirty years later.*

### James, the Mortician, recounts (1963)

It seems to me that I will never get back on my feet again. My notes are helpless attempts to revive the events of the past. Have I learned anything from that?

´You will survive us all´ Peter had told me before we left for the cemetery. And this time all of us were present. James instantly took up his position.

´I promised you to acquaint you with my view of things. More so, I want to disclose a secret. I have struggled with myself whether I should come clean with you. But it's no use.´

We all waited expectantly, Walter nodded at James invitingly.

´Well then, I am taking the plunge. After the funeral of the unknown girl I was unresponsive for a few days. I was alone, because my wife and my children were visiting the in-laws. I've always had the tendency to be a burden on myself.

Monologs were not unusual. I would probably have gone insane if my closest assistant had not approached me. He timbered the casket that the girl was buried in. On top of that he acted as gravedigger. He said in a low voice:

´I don't know if there's something to it. Just now there's an elderly man at the cemetery who claims he knew the young woman. He told me quite a few things. He doesn't know her name, but he does know her background.´

Hearing that story, I immediately hurried to the grave, but couldn't locate the man. For half an hour, I searched every nook and cranny of the cemetery to find him. My assistant took care of the customers in the meantime.

´Why didn't you tell me this earlier? The man is no longer there, vanished!´

He apologized to me, said it wasn't his fault. Not five minutes had passed when he had already notified me. I suspected the man had been pulling my leg. Though he might be my most valuable employee, he also had the tendency to exaggerate things, to describe them differently…I asked him whether he might possibly have just imagined this encounter? He denied this brusquely.

´Do you think I'm lying to you? Especially in a matter such as this? I know after all how strongly you are connected to the girl! May I drop dead if I have lied to you!´

I railed against my fate, locked myself into my office. Why had this person left without waiting for me? Had he taken fright?

James raised his hat. ´I think I have to take my leave for today. The memory is making me feel too melancholy.´

Walter grabbed his shoulders. 'No way, James! What you had to tell there is unbelievable! You finally just left the affair at that? Did you never have the idea to follow up on it, start a call, inform the press or whoever?'

We all more or less barged in. Will pushed James so vehemently against the chest that he lost his footing and fell on the ground.

'You humbugged us all, though you knew how much we suffered! How much would I have wished that this mysterious case was solved! And you were too cowardly to put your cards on the table!'

James picked himself up, brushed a little earth from his jacket and trousers.

'I understand your anger, Will. It would have been my and my employee's duty to report to the police with my employee. One year later, the whole thing repeated itself. My assistant immediately notified me that he had met the man again on the cemetery. This time he had even mentioned a name, which he however had not understood. Oh, and how fast did I run towards the grave. As fast as possible! From maybe 50 yards away I saw a figure that might be the crucial informant! Then I paused for a moment to recover from the strenuous running. When I looked up again, the figure had vanished. The man couldn't have gone far! He wasn't at the grave of the unknown girl. I surveyed the cemetery when I saw the figure! This time there was no time to lose. I advanced towards the man at a smart pace. And what can I say: the closer I got, the more familiar the man seemed to me. No wonder, I realized it was my employee, who obviously had been searching for the phantom himself! I have failed twice and the shame about it must be the reason that I let the whole matter rest. Today the whole thing sticks to me.´

No one spoke. We all started to move, in silent consent that in the face of this story, nothing more could be added. But James himself took a step towards us, folding his hands as if in prayer.

´I am sorry. I made a big mistake, burdened myself with guilt. My assistant described the stranger to me quite well. Based on his information it would have been quite possible to track him down. I probably didn't want the mystery to be revealed. Not much would have remained then of this uncanny story. Walter, you have described me too positively. I am not the philanthropist you take me for. Undoubtedly, it's a matter of importance to me to look after my fellow citizens, especially in my nature as a mortician. But there's this shadow of hate. I cannot bear to be rebuked. And if a person thinks he knows more than I do, I can turn into a lunatic. My soliloquies prove that I haven't yet found my own center. That's when I accuse myself of being unfit for society. Suicidal thoughts haunt me then. I am not worth bothering you with this story any longer. Forgive me!´

This time it was me who broke the silence that lasted several seconds.

´None of us is without sin. We all have incurred guilt. And it cannot be proved if the man actually knew the girl. Maybe he was just craving for approval, wanted to valorize his unappreciated existence...´

Peter took me home. It hadn't been arranged when the next meeting would take place. Was the reappraisal over now without any result and once and for all? And how should

Walter and Will rate the matter, who had taken such a long journey upon themselves to get to Willoughby?

*The bell sounded for the last days of Eduard Scherenschleifer's stay in Willoughby. He pulled himself from the mess of eternal regret at the last moment. His meetings with the by now 92-year old Karen, the apparently only contemporary witness still living in the place of the accident, were extremely precious and rewarding to him.*

## *A European in Willoughby, 2013*

Alfred had saved me from a fulminantly wrong decision. He once listened in by chance when I was having a very emotional phone call with my wife. Afterwards he took me aside. 'Don't make yourself unhappy, man! You know a little about my grandfather and how he nearly went insane. He would have given up everything for a young woman he had seen alive a single time. My grandmother suffered terribly. But it sorted itself out. He came to his senses, even though he could never forget the girl! My grandparents were together until his death. Nothing different has befallen you than what happens to all people who have a direct line to the other side. Stay with your family, don't destroy what you have built up.'

That hit home. I failed to understand myself anymore. My life had deteriorated into a nightmare that I was slowly waking from. One evening I called my wife. She didn't scold be, but instead cried heart-rendingly. I asked her for forgiveness. I wanted to be back in Vienna with her and the kids in a few days.

I read the records with slight scepticism. What was I to make of all this? I met with Karen. We ate apple pie and had coffee in the dining room of the retirement home.

'You have nothing to blame yourself for, young man! Everything is fine as it is. I bear the full responsibility for Josephine, there's nothing to be done about that. This here is nothing for you, it's a different world. We belong to the past, have lost sight of ourselves. That's what history has made of us. But the magic is the reward. It gives us the courage to believe in a better world. Humanity is on the point of exterminating itself. Maybe that isn't so wrong after all. A creature like Josephine seems to us as if escaped from a fairyland. She is a fairy that holds a wand in her hand. We marvel at her skills. She looks into our hearts, our souls. She is beyond our human weaknesses. The involvement with a creature beyond our imagination costs energy. But the magic is the reward, the magic is the reward!'

We set off towards the grave. The cemetery was devoid of people in the early evening. I sensed that this would be my last visit. Then I heard a voice penetrating me:

'I'm glad that we got to know each other. I wish you a good journey home!'

It wasn't Karen's voice. I prayed for the soul of the deceased.

I spent the next days without any expectations. I was looking forward to seeing my family again. The only important moments were the shared evenings with Karen. She told countless stories, exclusively stories that showed me how much in tune she was with Josephine. An old woman whose whole life seems to have been determined by a single encounter. I thank God that Alfred has led me back onto the right path. I will study the last pages of the records yet. Like any person, I fail at wanting to try to explain my life. It is good the way it is. What will be, will be. One must not think beyond that.

# THIRD PROTOCOL

Thanks to an article in the New Herald on the occasion of the 60$^{th}$ anniversary of the death of the "*Girl in Blue*" who is famous far beyond Willoughby and has gained notoriety, the ball has started rolling. It may be deemed a sensation that the victim's identity can be considered as clarified. The name of the young woman who was hit by a train and thus deceased on the 24$^{th}$ Dec. 1933 in Willoughby is Josephine Klimczak. She was the daughter of Jacob and Catherine Klimczak, who immigrated from Poland to Pennsylvania in 1901. Josephine was lovingly called Sophie by her family. She had five sisters and three brothers.

It has been already decided now by the local community to add a second headstone to the grave which will bear her name. The memories of a few contemporaries are coming alive again. They tell each other of the encounters they had with the girl. A few of them claim that she had appeared to them several times after her death, fresh as a daisy. Directly at the grave, in church, at a street corner, in a grove. Without doubt, these are cases of pipe dreams. Who would believe that Willoughby is haunted?

One thing is neither here nor there: why she travelled to Willoughby, what she wanted there, why she then rashly decided to take the train in the direction of New York, all these are questions that can probably never be answered. The mystery surrounding the death of Josephine Klimczak persists. Many a person still refuses to believe that she took her life or accidentally met her death. Crazed theories that she fell victim to a conspiracy or that a shadow with a devil's face pushed her in front of the train had boomed and are booming unabatedly.

Josephine Klimczak, the *"Girl in Blue"*, may she rest in peace! Especially now that the girl is a stranger no more, all kinds of rumors are spread, which ultimately cannot lead to any result. It is necessary to preserve the memory of a young woman for whom it was natural to treat her fellow human beings with courtesy and respect. Let us emulate her deeds and not go mad with wild speculations. Josephine will thank us sincerely.

*How do we humans handle memories? Does everything have to be about ourselves? Will, the former hobo, presented himself to the illustrious party at the grave of Josephine Klimczak as a profound person keen to unveil his thoughts about the possible survival of the "Girl in Blue".*

## Will, the literary scholar, recounts (1963)

Just two days after James's story, there was a knock on my door. It was Peter. He smiled at me, pointed outside.

´Nice weather today, isn't it?´ A remark that surprised me. But Peter instantly put his statement into perspective.

´Nice weather for a detour to the cemetery. Will came by this morning. The others have been informed already too. 3pm, is that ok with you?´

I felt a little taken by surprise, but nevertheless accepted immediately. I still had work to do. The household chores don't get done by themselves. As a single woman, I have grown used to being ensnared by men. Peter keeps on trying, makes eyes at me. Though he knows he has no chance with me. I finally arrived at the grave on time. We waited a few minutes for Walter, who clearly looked overtired. Will immediately began to speak.

῀I can only tell you how good it is for me to get it over with today. That's why I drove the long way here. I want to comment on Walter's play right away. Well written, no question. But I doubt that it contains more than one or two words of truth. No, don't be annoyed, my dear fellow. I am not done by far. The memory is the point. Who was I back then, who am I now? Day by day we humans are subjected to a process of change. We never are those we believe to be. As it was as far back as 25 years ago. I was young, believed to be superior to everybody else. And I was convinced to be able to solve the mystery surrounding the background of the death of this unknown girl. You have summoned us here because you are trying to free yourself from this girl. In fact, this is just a pretextual reason. You want to subject the memory of a girl to a metamorphosis, to enter into a different relationship with yourself. Let me talk a little about myself: I was bedazzled by the girl and thought never to be able to forget her. But a few weeks after her death I went my ways, took up my studies again. Today I am a literary scholar without permanent employment. I am my own master and in the face of this play I have asked myself whether I would be able to write about the events of that time. No, I can't, indeed, I cannot. The memory hasn't faded, but is stored within ourselves. Nothing is lost. But we humans each have different relations to our memories. For many years I repressed the calamity of Willoughby deep in my subconsciousness. There, it rested in peace. Only two, three years ago did I think of the records that Peter gave me to read back then. And everything was back. But just not the way it had happened. The reading glasses of the present see the past in a magnified way. What surfaces like a behemoth are small cuttings from a life that has long drifted onto a different track. I fail at the attempt to understand the past. The "*Girl in Blue*" has enchanted us all, for a few seconds we had the feeling of being kings and queens in a fairy-tale. Her death brought us back down to earth.´

No one even dared to breathe. From somewhere came the sound of construction noise.

´I spent five years in prison, I served my sentence. Before you get all nervous. It was a property crime, I had amassed a shitload of debts. Anyway, now I'm standing before you as a valuable member of society. I am reformed, have other priorities than 25, 30 years ago. Every day should be a celebration of life, today as well. What Walter is asking of us is impossible. Only he himself can cast off his chains that link him to the girl. It's all imagination after all. We believe to be taken in by something, yet we only want to bind ourselves to something so that we feel alive. Just stand back a little from yourself, Walter! Nowadays I am increasingly asking myself what would have become of the girl. She is nearly fifty years old, married, has three kids. She writes poems, is a needlework teacher. Her husband pampers her with flowers every few days, every year they travel to Europe for their holidays. She is always cheerful, loves life, believes in the good in man. She is a devout woman, regularly attends mass, prays fervently and is convinced that she will again see the loved ones that have preceded her in heaven. She is not a special person and exactly because of that she is special. She doesn't give herself airs, doesn't make anyone else responsible for her life. She sometimes thinks back to Willoughby, that she spent a glorious day in this little town. She recalls the people she wished a Merry Christmas. Her life proceeds in a calm, ordered way. She has no great expectations, she doesn't dream of a career, she delights in her two grandchildren. Yes, that is how I imagine her, she could have been such a woman today. Who knows how her life could have turned out. All our lives are but a short flicker. I can just reassure you that it feels good to warm the hearts of other people with these delicate flames. This girl did nothing else.´

´Is the famous grave of the "*Girl in Blue*" here?´ A middle-aged woman stood a little off and blinked in the direction of the grave.

´Famous grave, hm…´

Peter nodded. As if by command, we started to move. The woman looked after us.

´Your words have touched my soul´, I whispered to Will. He gave me a kiss on the brow.

´I am especially curious about your words, my dear.´

Before we all said goodbye, I cleared my throat. ´Tomorrow I will turn a little of myself inside out. Same time, same place.´

I had not planned to do my bit quite so fast. But I knew that above all, I owed it to myself to come clean. And delaying the matter wouldn't do me any good.

*Karen has accompanied us for long periods throughout the novel. Her fate particularly affects us. She did not get over the accident on Dec. 24th, 1933. The "Girl in Blue" rules her life till today. Thus, may her words, which she wrote down nearly 30 years after Josephine's death, cause a flood of associations.*

### Karen, the writer, remembers (1963)

My head was full of thoughts. I had no idea how much I should tell. Walter, Peter, James and Will had made no bones about it. What connected them was their search for a new life apart from the internal disturbance. I could and cannot keep up with that. I am affected to this very day. My imaginings constantly circle around the unknown girl. This can't be terminated. When I stand in front of her grave, I sometimes cry uncontrollably. Therapy with Peter did not bring about improvement of my dark thoughts. Why couldn't I emulate my closest allies? Perhaps it is like that because I was so young at the time of the accident. I have never recovered from my terrible dreams.

Instead, I became a writer. I have noted down for years what is going on inside me. It is difficult for me to put myself in other people's shoes, so I orientate on myself. My memories are alive. I have decided to follow in the girl's footsteps. Not that I could be like her! But my world is not mine. It is all so confused, unclear. Who am I? What am I torturing myself so much for? Could the truth set me free? I often rummage around in old records, but I don't find the truth there. I am trapped inside myself. The unknown young woman is not to blame. She is something like a refuge for my helplessness and reluctance to live. I could have learned so much from this girl! Instead I unabatedly suffered with her and for her. I lived and live, while she may possibly have fallen victim to a perfidiously planned crime. Will isn't interested anymore in solving the never even suspected criminal case. The story cannot be reconstructed any more. It is literally dead and buried. ´Let the dead rest in peace´, Peter told me again and again during therapy. He believed he was doing me a favor with that. Yes, there were moments when I felt free. Yes, the millstone was set aside, but it remained visible. And a second later, it was weighing on my soul again. I walked towards the cemetery like a frightened child.

´You can see that I am sick.´ That's the way I prefaced my speech. What followed was a nightmare. Each of my friends consoled me, comforted me. I wept bitterly. It was all too much. Walter invited me for a glass of wine. He excused himself for his egotism. He had thought only of his own problems. The tips of our fingers touched.

´I can't stay here´, he said with a broken voice. ´I can only hope that you won't take all of it to heart too much and can put the matter behind yourself someday. You'll be free then.´

Yes, freedom! My freedom is restricted to the writing of notes and the almost daily visit to a grave. Other than that, I am at my bookshop and do my time. I am my own worst enemy.

Well, and Walter's play? I haven't lost a word about it, especially as I am only mentioned in passing. My parents are an important part of the play. They are something like a poster couple that does everything right. Walter's wrong in this. The exterior façade all too often deceives. Neither my father nor my mother have ever understood me. They always posed and pose the wrong questions. The ideal family looks different. I wish for a different life. A life that starts with a sheltered childhood. Why didn't I manage to reveal the reason for my sadness, standing at the grave of the girl? Maybe I don't know myself why I never banned the demon whom I blamed for everything back then. I notice how my world threatens to collapse. It probably must. I should dare a new beginning. A new beginning that doesn't blame a *"Girl in Blue"* for a failed life. But am I able to do this? I look back and surrender responsibility.

Walter, Peter, James and Will met frequently. I fended off all invitations. And even if this was the last chance to rise again from the realm of the dead and take part in life, I did not want to grab it. I preferred to retreat. Sitting in my small room, I lamented my unjust fate. I had finished with earthly life. The unknown girl alone was my purpose in life and had been so for an eternity. Several times I had tried to put an end to my life. Always, I was saved in time. Then I spent weeks and months in a clinic. At last I was allowed back into the world. My brother took me in with his family, he touchingly took care of me. Sometimes we talked the whole night through until dawn. Carl even took leave from work to have more time for me. I am deeply indebted to him. If these records have any meaning, then it is to convey gratitude towards Carl. He knows me better than anyone else. Walter would maybe have married me, Will would have written a book about me, Peter would have made a therapeutic example of me, James would have held my eulogy after my successful suicide. But what am I writing…I am confused, not in my right mind. And I am sick. I have shouted out this truth and since then, they know it. Peter and James are good friends, but they recoil from my reticence. Only Carl is guessing what my inside looks like. He has never stopped assuming responsibility for his big sister. He is my anchor. And I am drifting on the endless seas and cannot find a shore where I could start a nicer, more meaningful life.

*It was necessary for Eduard Scherenschleifer to draw a summary about his insights he was able to gather in Willoughby. His stay had changed him. He would return to Vienna a different person. The records he had studied whole nights through no longer gave him headaches. He can live with the fact that the mystery of Willoughby will probably never be revealed.*

## *A European in Willoughby, 2013*

I strolled through town one more time, talked to people I encountered. Once more I collected impressions which shall continue to influence me for a lifetime I will never return to Willoughby. Never again see Josephine's grave. Those few days made a whole new person of me. I came closer to my true self. I cannot and will not think of Vienna. Bidding farewell to Karen and Alfred nearly broke my heart. But common sense prevails over sentiment. I would only be miserable in Willoughby in the long run.

    I won't sleep a bit this last night. Now I'm sitting at the desk and ponder what insights I can take with me. Life always turns out differently than you think. A change has manifested itself inside me from yesterday to today. Maybe my family will have difficulties handling it. I won't slip back into the boring life. A lot will not be part of my life any more.

The journey back will last an eternity. No one will accompany me, but those people to whom I owe a deep debt of gratitude will forever find a place in my heart. The inquiries did not lead to the result I desired. What the death of Josephine Klimczak is all about will probably never be solved. But I have learned to respect the unknown. This young woman has enriched the life of many people. The magic radiating from her is so strong that it even impresses people today. I have received a tiny share of that magic.

Why did Josephine spend her last hours in Willoughby? There is no ´coincidence´, at least I am convinced of that. Therefore, it was supposed to happen the way it did. My wish to desperately go searching for clues in Willoughby has come true. I almost paid a very high price. Maybe I will leave a tiny gap.

Who now was that quirky guy with the funny accent? I am growing ever more tired. Maybe I should at least lie down, even if I won't be able to sleep. And when I wake up, I will have dreamed of Josephine. She will watch over me as a guardian angel, so that I'll also arrive in Vienna unscathed.

*I can only whole-heartedly thank my narrator, who was willing to fulfil my assignment. He was closer to the dead than to the living in those days of the year 2013. Death proved to be the main topic in this phase of his life, which can also be discerned from the story around the*

*"Girl in Blue". I don't know how he is doing nowadays. Maybe he is already conversing with Josephine in the ultimate reality.*

### *The Narrator, 2013*

My characters will survive me, that may be the only solace available to me. When a book, a novella, a novel has been written, the finished work separates itself from the author. It gains a life of its own. As long as people engage with them out of their free will, the characters are filled with life. The narrator stands somewhere in the background, dreaming of a new story. I will come to an end. But the culmination takes place at a point in time which I don't determine myself. Death is waiting for me, he is coming closer and closer. Day by day I look him in the eye. Overcoming fear of death does not play any role in my stories. My characters act like immortals. When I look back, I only recognize patchwork. I have nothing to do anymore with the person who was ready to implement the idea of a story. Too much has happened in the meantime. Thousands, hundreds of thousands of events have turned me into a person who is heading towards himself. Where am I at this moment? The distance ahead of me is far shorter than the distance already travelled. I don't need to look into a crystal ball to imagine my future. I had my fortune told just once. That was nearly seven decades ago. I can still remember the prophecy exactly: you will do what you are destined for.

With that, everything has been said what all people should try to accomplish for themselves. To become who they are. I have often taken shortcuts, made wrong decisions. But towards the end of my life I am not blaming myself for anything anymore. This *"Girl in Blue"* has enraptured me. There was no turning back. I wanted to walk in her footsteps without coming into contact with her. No human life will risk being unmasked. Those people who witnessed Josephine personally sensed a little of who this young woman might have been. I, as a non-participant, put on a mask and dived into the infinitely deep sea of my subconscious where my characters were waiting to get in touch with the everyday life of Willoughby. A daily life that was severely shaken by an incomprehensible event.

Edi felt like an unhappy king in this town of his yearning. He was ready to leave his old life behind and devote his new life to a long-dead girl. Like his creator, he was groping in the dark. The study of contemporary letters and reports let that light flare up which had driven him to Willoughby. Only Karen symbolized the reality behind the story. She showed herself both on and behind the stage.

One thing remains to be told. I will not be able to thus solve the puzzle. But I must free myself for the enchanting life. I can only do that by letting my characters roam free in their world. They will grow a little with every reader who imagines them.

*What was bestowed on Karen on her 80th birthday, therefore more than 67 years after her single encounter with Josephine, turned out to be the most wonderful present she ever received. She will tell this story to every person she meets unto the day she dies. Quite a few petrified hearts can be broken and restored by it.*

### Carl talks about the magic of Willoughby, 2001

Time flew by and I became an old woman. I celebrated my 80th birthday with Carl. He had brought me a birthday cake on which just a single candle was stuck. We hugged. On that day he told me a lot about his family, which was no longer intact. His wife had run off decades ago, his kids had since led their own lives. This did not change his positive attitude towards life. When dusk had fallen, and I expected him to leave me soon, he dug out some sheets of handwritten paper from his backpack.

'This is just for you, Karen! The background to these records is a short one. Nearly three years ago I met a man in the cemetery. A very old man, maybe even a hundred years old. Who knows if he is even still alive. This man saw me standing at Josephine's grave. He patted me on the back, then put these sheets into my hand. He did not speak a word. Neither do I want to comment on them. You have to let the legend sink in, must not shy back from it. It might have happened thus, if we believe in things that our mind cannot fathom.' I was ready to listen to Carl's voice, completely focused.

'Josephine was a cheerful child. She liked to play with dolls, loved to indulge in daydreams, grew up in an extended family with many siblings who thrived just like her. Mother and father fulfilled her every wish, if it was in their power. A childhood, the likes of which was rare. At last she had matured into a young woman and not a day had passed on which she had not been grateful for the beauty of the world and the uniqueness of her life. Then a young woman with a brilliant smile addressed her in the street.

"You have incurred guilt and I am cursing you for it. When I have vanished, you will lead a life as a female dog. Not a day will pass which won't make you long for death. Because your happiness has now come to an end."

Josephine didn't take the enchanting young woman's words seriously. Nevertheless, she wanted to say a friendly goodbye as she had always done. But she couldn't utter a single word. Her voice failed her. And then she noticed that the curse had come true. She was looking down at furry front legs. A dog! She wanted to scream, but nothing more than an angry yapping materialized. She spent those first days of her dog's life hoping that she would spend her time only temporarily like that. The woman would surely show up again and realize that she had made a mistake. Because which guilt should she have incurred? She thought about it hard, but nothing came to mind. After a week she encountered other dogs which played in a garden. She ran to the fence that separated her from the other dogs. The dogs took one look at her, retreated soon afterwards. In the coming months she also was ignored by other dogs. Wherever she encountered other dogs, they turned away. She was a dog whose life made no sense.

Day by day she pondered why she had to endure such a severe punishment. She ran many miles and had moved away from her home town long ago. Her parents and siblings surely were very worried about her. After half a year the sorceress appeared to her again. She took her in her arms. The sorceress stroked her fur.

"Well, young lady, you wouldn't have imaged that, huh? As you have noticed, you cannot be happy as a dog. The other dogs know that you're not one of them. You have a scent that disgusts them. Do you want to lead this unworthy life for all eternity? There is a way out, don't worry! I am giving you the chance to be human for one more day. You can weigh the pros and cons; what means more to you: languish as a dog in eternal damnation or enjoy a last nice day as a human being! But allow me to point out that this last day will end with your death. I don't know what will happen afterwards, maybe death is a door into another world where you don't have to suffer any more. It is within my power to release you from your canine existence."

Josephine looked sadly at the woman. She thought that her life as a dog had long since broken her heart. If she was at least a dog that could play with her same species and experience adventures! But that was not granted to her, for whatever reasons…

"As I said then, you have incurred guilt! You caged my best friend and let her die miserably of starvation and thirst."

All of sudden Josephine knew what this was about. When a small girl, maybe eight or nine years old, her parents had given her a hamster. She promised to take care of this hamster. But for a few days, she forgot to feed it and also didn't put down a little bowl of water for it. When she saw it lie dead in its cage, she screamed in horror. That happened so many years ago. She had regretted it deeply, but apparently that hadn't sufficed.

"Very good that you can remember so well, young lady! The punishment I am imposing on you might seem overly cruel to you. But life isn't just a collection of nice moments, sometimes the devil himself takes hold of a person. The same with you. You were just a child and erased the life of an innocent being. Your bad luck is that Thelma was my best friend. She once had been a human too, who had incurred guilt. And you won't believe me when I tell you that it's not different with myself. It is my duty as sorceress to punish people for their crimes until all eternity. This is because I once killed someone myself. Whoever kills someone must not enjoy the pleasures of life for the duration of their lifetime and beyond. I cannot help it, I got this destiny without having had a choice. If I am offering you a last day as a human being, it is an act of mercy which you should seize. There's nothing more I can do for you, and it is by no means the case that I am granting this chance to all people that have been cursed by me!"

After these explanatory words Josephine was split. She pondered how she should decide. Quickly, much faster than anticipated she realized that life as a human being had meant a lot to her. To be cursed for an eternity and, as a dog, to be always searching for a meaning that could never be found... She chose human life. Instantly she delighted in her human form which was granted to her again. She touched her nose, rubbed her eyes, looked at her feet, which were stuck in too tight shoes. From now on she had 24 hours to enjoy her existence as a young woman to the full.´

´A church clock struck ten times. She didn't know which city she was in. Right in the vicinity she discovered a bus terminal. She inquired when the next bus was leaving. >You'll have to hurry! In five minutes, to Willoughby!< She bought a ticket. A suitcase which didn't seem to belong to anyone stood in the middle of the street. She took it, then entered the bus. The ride started right on time. Only now did she breathe deeply. If what the woman had told her was correct, then her life would be over in a few hours' time. Had it all been a dream? Her existence as a dog an imagination? And how could it be that she had been so severely punished? Yes, she had incurred guilt as a child, but she believed in mercy! What kind of world is this, if every insignificant offense has such consequences for the individual? The bus reached Willoughby only the next morning. Josephine hadn't been able to sleep for a second. She thanked the bus driver for the safe journey. Then she stood hesitantly in the street. A man addressed her, but she wasn't in the mood to spend the near future in company. There remained almost exactly 16 hours of lifetime for her, thus every minute must be fully enjoyed. She began to walk and came to a halt a few minutes later in front of a guest house. A middle-aged woman seemed to have been waiting for her. She opened the door and let Josephine enter.

>I want to rest for an hour or so<

The proprietress nodded. The room was simple, but lovingly furnished. She put the suitcase down on the bed and opened it. The only contents were a white blouse, blue shoes, a little blue jacket and a blue skirt. Everything fitted like a glove, as if it had been made for her! Did the crazy sorceress with an especially cruel form of death for her? No, that must be prevented! A train approached the grove. That's when she began to run. She ran and ran and ran…She had never run this fast in her whole life. She took one big step. A single tear wet her cheek. Even before the train hit her, she was in the other world.´

*Our novel has now come to an end. What will forever remain are the questions that those people pose themselves for whom the 24th of December 1933 is not a random date. With that day, a new era began in Willoughby, which still has a lasting effect until today and in the future, far across the borders of the small town.*

have something to do with it? Be that as it may, she rested for a few minutes, lying down on the bed. Her thoughts were with her family, whom she would never see again. Only then did she notice the calendar on the wall.

"Today is the 24th of December!", she nearly screamed out loud. Today of all days the 24th of December! That day which was especially dear to her. Just the day for dying, she thought. She wouldn't live to see Christmas Mass, so she got up and set out for the nearby church.

In church she prayed for nearly an hour. She thanked the Lord for a wonderful, happy, only rarely sad life. Her demise should be painless. She was looking forward to seeing loved ones again soon. And she asked for forgiveness of her sins. Her thoughts had not always been pure, some things she would have liked to undo. But she did not quarrel with her fate, but wanted to prepare herself for paradise. As soon as she had left the church, she encountered people, whom she all greeted with a smile in her heart and whom she wished a happy and spiritual Christmas. With one or the other she exchanged a few more words. People showed themselves to be amenable and friendly, they opened their hearts for a few moments and she saw that those children she met were of a purer heart than hers.

With every passing minute her lifetime dwindled. That is the case with every creature. With the difference that she knew in advance when she had to die. The time passed quickly, soon the church clock struck nine times. She sat on a tree stump close to the train station. No human being was close to her. Now and then there was a rustling in this grove. Then she saw the sorceress in front of her. Just a few minutes, then Josephine would die. She wasn't afraid of death, but she did not want to be surprised. What if the sorceress had come up